ROOM THIRTY

A CLUB SIN NOVELLA

MAE HARDEN

This is a work of fiction. Names, characters, businesses, places, events, locales, and incidents are either the products of the author's imagination or used in a fictitious manner. Any resemblance to actual persons, living or dead, or actual events is purely coincidental.

Cover art by Mae Harden

Developmental and Line Editing by Kraken Communications

Copyright © 2022 Mae Harden

All rights reserved. This book or any portion thereof may not be reproduced or used in any manner whatsoever without the express written permission of the author except for the use of brief quotations in a book review.

Published in the United States of America 2021

www.maeharden.com

*For all the readers who asked for more dirty talk...
You're welcome.*

P.S. - Mom, if you're reading this, turn back NOW.

Club Sin Rules

Upon entering Club Sin, you are consenting to the following:

1. You are STI/STD free.
2. You are healthy and able to engage in or observe sexual activity at Club Sin.
3. You are on or have brought birth control of your choice.
4. You consent to engage in the kink of your choice upon entering the room of your choice. Anyone is welcome in the room that represents their kink with consent; privacy is maintained when requested. Multiple partners are common and encouraged at Club Sin.
5. No kink shaming allowed. People are free to explore and enjoy all their desires in a safe and consensual environment at Club Sin.
6. Honesty and communication are key to a satisfying experience at Club Sin.
7. Discretion and privacy are valued at Club Sin.
8. No cell phones are allowed in Club Sin.
9. Universal safe word at Club Sin is RED, unless otherwise agreed upon. Be aware of non-verbal cues.

At Club Sin we want you to have a satisfying experience. Go and play!

1

BRIELLE

"Yeah, I'm like, super into rowing. It's a men's only crew though. No offense, but women just can't keep up and I like to go *hard*. Gotta stay in shape, right?" The stomach-turning frat boy masquerading as a man winks at me, the innuendo decidedly not subtle. The thing is, that was probably the least offensive thing he's said about women all night.

Brad leans his elbow on the table and gives his wrist a shake. He's been doing it all night, forcing me to look at the gaudy watch strapped around his wrist. If this bozo really wants me to comment on his knock-off Piaget, he's going to have to ask for it, and he's not going to like what I have to say. The cheap imitation was probably made by children paid pennies a day, if they were even paid at all. Every time I look at the thing, it makes bile rise in my throat, much like the man sporting it.

I don't respond to the double entendre. I really couldn't care less how 'hard' he goes with his 'crew' or the new shell his daddy bought him.

What kind of grown man still talks like this? *One who*

had everything handed to him, I think. Leaning back in my chair, I try to subtly get our server's attention, resisting the urge to roll my eyes as Brad prattles on about river conditions this week.

Gag. I really should have bailed the second he ordered for me without even bothering to ask what I wanted. But his family is connected, and it won't do me, or my company, any favors to be a raging bitch, no matter how much he deserves it.

Chicago is a big city, but the high rollers do their rolling together, and they are petty as fuck. Bringing on the ire of any of the old-money families could be enough to sink my little fledgling. Still, I'd give my left ovary to get out of here.

Brad is engrossed in the dessert menu, telling me which ones he wants to share. Does he offer me a choice? Does he offer me my own dessert? Of course not. And I never expected him to. Not after he looked me up and down and declared me "curvier" than his "normal girls." My left eye hasn't stopped twitching ever since. God forbid my ribs don't jut out.

The server finally glances in my direction, and I mouth 'check', eyes flashing as I wag a hundred-dollar bill by my hip, down out of Brad's sight. It's crumpled and sweaty. I snuck it out of my purse fifteen minutes ago, and I've been clutching it between angry fingers ever since.

It's taken the server a hot minute to catch on, but it's all his if he moves his ass and brings the check. His eyes go wide in his baby face and, like a freaking wizard, he apparates by my side in under a minute, the leather folder tucked against his side. He moves to set it on the table, but I take it, quickly tucking the Benjamin inside, along with my credit card, and handing it right back.

"Hang on," Brad says, finally catching on. The waiter freezes, eyes darting between the two of us. "I thought we were going to split a cheesecake." My date pouts. He actually pouts. If he was five, I might give a shit. But at 35, there's no excuse for pouting like that.

"I have an early morning," I say, forcing my expression into what I hope looks like a disappointed grimace. "We're all set," I say to the waiter, dismissing him. He doesn't need to be told twice, and turns on his heel, scampering away before Brad can hold him up again.

"You should have at least let me pay," he grumbles.

Ha. No. I know exactly how men like him think. If I let him pay, he's going to think I owe him something. And without fail, that something is sex. I'd rather carve my own eyeballs out with a melon baller than let this douche get in my panties.

"That's okay," I say, my fragile politeness wearing ever thinner. "It's not like I can't afford to pay for my own meals." I can't help getting the little jab in. It's true, too. My sustainable, fair-trade clothing company is blowing up. Growth at an unprecedented pace—that's what our last financial report read. My net worth may not match his family's wealth, but I built it from the ground up.

I can see the wheels turning behind Brad's dull eyes, grinding along at a glacial speed. I wonder if he was always this vapid or if a lifetime of handouts and undeserved praise turned him into... this.

"Well, let me pay next time." *Because Og is Man! Og pay for weak female. Og deserve pussy.* He doesn't say the last part out loud, but it's layered in there with that caveman tone of his. I grit my teeth, suppressing the urge to tell him where to shove his toxic masculinity, but he still hasn't caught on.

"Whatever. Let's get out of here. I could use a nightcap." Brad winks at me again and runs the rough edge of his shoe up my bare calf. The pain isn't what pisses me off. It's the blatant disrespect. The ass-hattery of his assumptions. At no point in this entire miserable evening did I say one thing that would lead him to believe I'd want to go home with him. The lion, the witch, and the *audacity* of this bitch.

What part of 'I have an early morning' doesn't he get? His complete lack of social awareness makes me want to bury my face in my hands and scream. Just… wow. Is he really that stupid or does he think I'll go home with him if he keeps pretending this has gone well? I'm leaning toward stupid.

And selfish.

If the one-sided conversation over the last hour is anything to judge by, I'd bet a million bucks he's a two-pump chump in bed who thinks buying me half a dessert is plenty of foreplay. I'm already standing when the waiter brings my credit card back. I slip another hundred in his palm as I take my card and scribble my name on the bill.

I head toward the door, not bothering to see if Brad is following. I really couldn't care less. I just want to go home, get the hell out of these heels, and drown my loneliness in a bottle of expensive red wine. And chocolate. I deserve chocolate.

My alarm goes off at 6 am. There's a soft whirring as the automatic shades lift, exposing skyline views of downtown Chicago. There's a hint of light coming from the east, but the sun has at least half an hour to go before the golden glow spills through the space. I make my coffee and step out onto the balcony, settling into my favorite chair to catch up on emails.

When JustCloth went big, it went BIG. And it did it almost overnight. One celebrity plug on the red carpet and a four-minute feature on the morning news was all it took. I think it was a 'right idea, right time' situation more than anything. For every clothing company that picks up a solid following, there are hundreds that go nowhere.

But we got lucky, and I wasn't about to squander it. We worked day and night for months, sourcing new items, building up the infrastructure, and fitting out extra warehouses to keep up with demand. I went days at a time without sleeping, but I pulled through. We pulled through —and we didn't just keep up. We thrived.

After months of crashing on my office couch or passing out face down on my desk, I spoiled myself. No more rat-infested studio apartments on the edge of the city, with their leaky pipes and weird smells. It's been six months, and I still don't miss the trumpet quartet that lived, and practiced, in the unit above me.

This condo came at a premium, but the walls are gloriously soundproofed, and waking up to watch the sunrise over downtown makes my Chicagoan heart sing.

I wrap up a few loose ends before getting ready to head to the office. I carefully tuck a cream-colored silk blouse into my black pencil skirt. My long, black hair goes up in the same French twist I wear every day. My stylist always tries to cut little pieces in the front to 'soften' the look, but I don't have time to fuss with it. I do my makeup, keeping it natural-looking. But even that requires a ton of work.

"It's almost Friday, girl. You got this," I mutter as I

smudge out soft brown eyeliner. I love my company. I love my employees (most of them anyway). I love working. But fourteen-hour days stack up fast and take their toll, physically and mentally. By the time I get to the weekend, I have a *lot* of steam to blow off.

I hail a cab and climb inside. I don't like working in moving cars, so I let my mind wander and count it as meditation time. Meditating today mostly consists of brainstorming ways to blow off the aforementioned steam.

Kickboxing works. Mostly.

There's always clubbing. I'm not a party girl by any stretch. I'm not a heavy drinker, and I never liked the way party drugs made me feel. What does it for me is the dancing. The body-vibrating music, the crush of bodies, the fever pitch the crowd reaches, roiling like a living entity… that calms me in a way I can't explain.

But it doesn't make my toes curl. It doesn't wrap around me as I sleep, or go for leisurely brunches with me on Sundays.

2

BRIELLE

These are the absolute worst. I throw the mock-ups back down on my desk and hit the intercom button. "Kelly, bring me the marketing department."

"All of them?" she replies, peeking her head through the door. I nod wordlessly. "Oh, are you going to yell at them?" she asks, her tone gleeful. "If you do, can I watch?"

I laugh. This is why I love my assistant. Her cut-throat attitude always catches me off-guard. With her sweet face, silky blonde hair, and girl-next-door vibe, it's easy to forget that she grew up in inner-Chicago and throws a left hook like I've never seen. Even my kickboxing instructor was intrigued, and he's not easily impressed.

"Absolutely. I want them here asap. Oh, please call security. Tell them we're likely to have five terminations, and I need them up here now."

Kelly nods and bounces out of my office like I told her there's ice cream in the break room. I stare down at the storyboards and advertising mock-ups the marketing team left on my desk, my molars grinding audibly. This is the final straw. I've been patient. I've tried to steer them in the right direction, but this is just gross, and I can't do their job for them anymore.

Mom guilt is real! But with JustCloth denim, there's one less thing to feel bad about... Carpool is hard, our jeans aren't... Your husband can have his tools, the only thing you need is JustCloth.

"Sexist bullshit," I mutter. This campaign is un-fucking-believable. How in god's name could they think this copy is appropriate for any company, let alone a woman-run company, selling women-made clothes? The graphics are even worse. In one particularly infuriating mockup, they have a cheesy before and after with what I can only describe as lumpy pancake butt, and a wildly over-edited image of an obscenely unrealistic bubble butt.

They've been working on this campaign for weeks. How much money did I waste just so they could take our marketing back to 1952? My heart is pounding in my temples, my blood seething. There's an authoritative knock, and before I even say, 'come in', my office door swings open. Kevin, the head of marketing comes swaggering in, a grin on his punchable face. A mother-fucking-grin.

His four employees trail after him, looking slightly less confident, but certainly not as worried as they should be. Kelly scoots in after them, shutting the door. Eyes bright, she takes a seat in one of the armchairs by the floor-to-ceiling windows, a notebook open on her lap and a pen poised to take notes.

Not that we need notes. There will be no more corrections. There will be no more warnings. And, after I'm finished with them, there will be five vacancies in marketing.

"So, this is what you're presenting? Walk me through

it." I say, my voice intentionally gentle. Curious even, which is really hard to do when I want to rip them each a new asshole.

Kevin gives me a smarmy smile. Maybe it's residual anger over my 'date' last night, but I have had it with guys like this. "Well, we went tongue in cheek. Retro," he explains like I'm five years old. I don't say a word, just let him keep talking; let him hang himself with his own rope.

"Market research shows women want to be cared for, pampered. Moms and young to middle aged professionals are our corner demographic, and they're tired. Exhausted."

I want to cackle. What does Mr. Ducks-out-after-30-hours-a-week know about exhausted? But the men behind him nod like this is perfectly fine. I pick up the Mom-Guilt ad, tapping my nail against the board it's mounted on.

"Who came up with this one?" I ask, voice light, face an expressionless mask. Kelly is practically trembling with excitement. She knows what's coming down the line, and after seeing these boards, I know she's just as appalled as I am.

One of the guys in the back raises his hand, looking far too proud of himself. "Uh… that was me. My wife is always bitch—er, moaning about how tired she is after watching our four kids all day. Complains about mom-guilt all the time."

I nod like that wasn't one of the most disgusting things I've ever heard, and pick up the carpool ad. "And this one?" Kevin still looks like a smug shit, but the guys behind him exchange glances, their shoulders dropping ever so slightly.

The guy in the middle, Haden or Kaden, or something like that, raises his hand timidly. I can't keep the hard, bubbling anger out of my expression any longer. I hold up the carpool storyboard, the one meant to be a video ad for social media. I don't have to say anything. One by one, I tap on the boards, noting who made what. By the time I've gotten through the stack, Kevin's face has fallen. But instead of looking ashamed, there's anger in his eyes.

"So let me get this straight, all five of you thought this campaign was a good idea?" No one nods or says a word, but they don't deny it either.

"The research—" Kevin blusters, but I interrupt.

"I've seen the research, Kevin. I read it front to back. Three times. Something you clearly failed to do. You cherry-picked bits to back up this sexist garbage instead of putting the whole picture together. In fact, you *all* completely missed the entire point of those reports. Which, I'd like to add, we paid out the nose for. This," I hold up the pile of storyboards and mockups, making sure they all see it. "This is worse than trash."

"Now, hang on." Kevin raises his voice, yelling over me. "It's a joke. It's supposed to be funny. You just don't get it because you're an uptight bitch!"

Kelly giggles in the corner, knowing what a huge mistake that was. All five of the men glance in her direction, alarmed by her outburst. But I love it. If I could let my guard down right now, I would have laughed at that comment too. Not because it's funny, but because it really was the single stupidest thing he could have blurted out.

A smile spreads over my face. It's cold, but it's what they deserve. Leaning back against my desk, I cross my arms. "I hired you on a recommendation, Kevin. Clearly that was a mistake. As was letting you pick your own staff." I eye the group of straight, white, middle-aged men. I can't say it out loud, but he hobbled this team by limiting the voices and perspectives. "The echo-chamber is done. You're fired."

Kevin turns beet red, his face going splotchy as the anger visibly colors his skin all the way down to his shirt collar. "You can't fuck me like that!" He grits out through snarled lips. He takes a step toward me. The hair rises on the back of my neck at the vitriol in his voice. My muscles tense, and I signal Kelly to show security in. They all watch her stand and leave the office.

"Kevin," I say, forcing a bored tone. "I wouldn't fuck you if you were the last man on earth. Because even then, you'd still be disgusting. Now. Get. Out."

Seven security guards file into the room, one of them coming to stand between Kevin and I, a stern expression on his face. He gestures for Kevin to leave the room. My *former* head of marketing mutters a hateful diatribe the whole way out, leaving the four remaining members of the marketing team to gawk at me. Between them, the six guards keeping them in line, and Kelly watching with wide eyes, my airy office has never felt so cramped.

I stare back at the marketing team—the ex-marketing team—but they don't leave. Then it hits me.

"Oh, I'm sorry, did you think I was just talking to Kevin?" I ask. Their eyes dart between me, security, and each other nervously. "I'll say it slowly. You're *all* fired. Security will escort you to collect your personal belongings."

They grumble and swear under their breath, but they file out of my office. The guards trail after them to ensure they turn in their key cards and don't steal company property.

I sink into my chair, mentally willing the mockups to burst into flames, but they don't. So, I sweep them into my tiny trash can and stomp on them with my heel to make them fit.

It occurs to me that we are now wildly behind schedule. I need a new marketing team. Like, now. "Kelly!" I call out, forgetting to use the intercom. We didn't have an intercom when it was just a couple of us working out of a dingy warehouse, and I'm still getting used to it.

My assistant pops her head through my door. "That was freaking awesome, Bree." She glides back into my office and takes a seat across from me.

"Thanks. It felt a little brutal."

"Hell no. They needed to go. You know Kevin hit on me in the break room the other day?"

"What?" I sit up straight, teeth grinding again.

"Stop that! You're going to need dentures by the time you're forty." I'm not one hundred percent sure if she's concerned about my molars, or if she just straight up hates teeth grinding. Either way, she's not wrong. "Anyways, it's fine, I kneed him in the nuts. By accident."

"Accident?" I ask with a grin. "Never mind, don't answer that. We need to hire out marketing until I can get a new team in place. Can you do some sleuthing?"

Kelly practically sparkles. Sleuthing is her specialty. "Tell me what you want, and I'll find it," she says, sitting taller in her chair.

"Okay… look for a boutique marketing firm. No big houses. Bonus points for firms that specialize in social marketing. Keep it quiet. I really don't want it getting out that I canned the entire department in one go."

Kelly scribbles on her notepad and hops up. "You got it," she says cheerfully. I glance at the clock as she leaves. Jesus. 9:53 am. That's it? I sigh and open my email, ready for round two. But my fingers freeze, hovering over my keyboard. At the top of my inbox is a message I've been waiting for. I click on it, my heart racing.

To: Brielle Guerrero
From: C.S. Entertainment
Subject: Welcome

Good morning Ms. Guerrero,

Thank you for your patience. Your application has been approved and your vetting complete. We are pleased to welcome you to Club Sin…

There are rules and procedures to read through, but I have to pause and catch my breath. Club Sin. Room after room of fantasies to lose myself in. A palace devoted to sexual fulfillment. I shiver just thinking about it. I've been on a dry spell for so long, I almost can't remember what sex is like with an actual person. My vibrator collection is epic, but it's not the same.

I struggle through my day, something I never do, but the itch to get out of here, to brave a new adventure keeps growing. I keep looking back at the email, losing an hour of productivity every single time. Because then I start Googling.

What do you wear to a sex club? What do you wear to a kink club? Sex club safety. How to approach a dom. How do you tell if someone is a dom? Ice cream delivery near me.

That last one was the inevitable end of my searches. Once the overwhelming landslide of internet advice became too much, ice cream seemed like the only logical choice. I've refrained from ordering about six pints today, and that alone should earn me a pat on the back.

Or… a good spanking? I bite my lip and glance at the time. Again. 4:02. I tap my foot, watching the sleek little digital clock on my desk. Still 4:02. I would swear up and down that the damn thing is broken if it didn't match my wristwatch, phone, and computer.

"Kelly!" I holler, getting to my feet. She doesn't answer, but then I remember that I sent her on a mission. Doesn't matter. I've never played hooky a day in my life, but today is the day. I collect my things, dumping them unceremoniously into my bag, and go looking for my assistant.

I don't have to go far. Kelly is sitting at her desk, headphones in, as she sends out feelers via email. I tap her on the shoulder, and she jumps, spinning her chair to face me as she yanks her headphones out.

"Are you okay?" She eyes my purse warily. "You don't have any meetings today. Are you sick?"

"I'm fine," I reassure her. "I just need to take care of some personal stuff."

Kelly looks at me like I've lost it. "Personal stuff? Okay body snatcher, where'd you hide my boss?"

"Very cute," I retort, unable to hold my grin back. "I know, but honestly, I'm just not feeling it today." She watches me leave, one eyebrow about an inch higher than the other.

I'm dying to get to Club Sin. This is it. I can feel it. The era of dating is done, at least it is for me. I don't need romance. I don't need or want a man to look after me. I just need to scratch an itch, and if there's one place in the city I can find someone to scratch me, it's Club Sin.

3

LEO

I speed walk through the lobby, nodding at Carl, the security guard. He looks at his watch and gives me an "oh shit" look. I'm late. I'm always late. Mal hates when I'm late. Thorin… he doesn't care. As long as I get everything done, it doesn't bother him if I'm less of a nine-to-five guy and more of an eleven-to-the-middle-of-the-night partner.

Slinging my cross-body laptop bag behind my back, I dash up the stairs, taking the steps two at a time. The elevator takes fucking forever in this building. I pause outside our office, panting just a bit as I straighten my tie.

"You're late." Thorin's gruff voice makes me jump. I turn to eye him. Jeans, t-shirt, leather jacket. That's his uniform. But the bag slung over his shoulder tips me off.

"You're one to talk. At least I got here before you."

He grins and pushes me forward. I smack his hand and open the door. Gladys waves at me from reception. Normally I'd stop and say hi, but Thorin puts his hands on my shoulders, steering me toward the office we share with Mal.

We tried working in a conventional office space, each of us in our own corners with doors and intercoms and everything. But that's just not our process. We moved back and forth between the offices all day long, running from one place to another and, in the end, we ended up working in the break room every day.

When the three of us split off to open our own agency, the open office space was Thorin's idea, and I have to admit, it was a good one. After years of corporate work, it felt wrong giving up the corner office I worked so hard to get, but this is better. Plus, it still has that fresh paint smell.

Mal's at his desk, no surprise there. What *is* shocking is his lack of response to our tardy arrival. We usually get scolded like kids who skipped homeroom, but not today. He's typing furiously, eyes glued to the screen. He hears us though, because he raises one finger, forbidding us to interrupt him.

Thorin shrugs and tosses his jacket at the overflowing coat rack. It hangs on—barely—making him grin like an idiot. He sets his motorcycle helmet in its dedicated cubby and heads to the Keurig.

I'm too curious about whatever Mal is buried in over there. Sneaking up behind him, I read the email over his shoulder.

…immediately thought of you three. They want a boutique marketing firm. Small and focused on socials…

"That sounds promising," I whisper, making Mal jump in his chair.

"God dammit. Why do you insist on sneaking around like that?" he growls, making Thorin laugh.

"I can't help it if I'm light-footed." I shrug. "We can't

all be as stompy as you." Lifting my chin toward the screen I ask, "Scroll up, what's the company?"

"No clue," Mal grumbles, giving us an annoyed look as Thorin comes to read over his shoulder too. "You jackasses were CC'd, go read it at your own desk."

"Why?" Thorin grins. "You've already got it pulled up."

"Well, they won't tell me the name of the company." He shuts his monitor off.

"So?" I ask.

"So, I'm not going to a meeting blind."

"It's a *client*," I remind him. "You know, those people who pay the bills and keep the lights on?" Mal rolls his eyes, but even he can't be that rigid. "Mal, seriously. Set the meeting. We're taking it. I don't care if they want us to hock electric cock rings, we need this."

He doesn't answer, but I watch as he opens the laptop back up and hits the reply all button. "This better not be electric cock rings," he growls.

"Maybe it's not!" I tell him cheerfully, smacking him on the back.

I'm at my desk hours later, re-touching a stock image, pixel by painful pixel, when Mallon's voice booms through the office. "Our mystery meeting is set at five pm tomorrow evening. There you go! I put it on the calendar!" His tone is decidedly salty, but we need all the clients we can get. "You're welcome!"

"Thank you!" I call back.

Thorin gets to his feet, stretching loudly. "I need to blow off some steam."

I lean back in my chair, ears perking up. I could definitely blow off some steam. "Sin?" I ask. He nods, raising his eyebrows at Mal, already shuffling his papers into a messy stack.

"So, you're just going to have a seven-hour workday?" he asks. I'm ahead on everything, and I know Mal is too, but that doesn't stop him from being a dick.

"You want to sit and stare at the wall for the next hour? Or do you want to go find a rope bunny and spend the rest of the night making her come?"

Mallon clicks his monitor off, getting to his feet before I can even save and close my project. "You make a valid argument," he says, heading toward the exit.

4

MALLON

I sip my gin and tonic, barely tasting it. Thorin elbows me in the side. "Dude, get your mopey ass together."

"Aren't you just sweet and sensitive tonight," I say wryly.

"No work. Not here."

I roll my eyes at my stepbrother. "Just because you have a steel partition in your brain doesn't mean the rest of us do. I don't like it."

Thorin huffs. "It'll be fine. It's a time and an address. They can't possibly expect a presentation if they won't even tell us the company name. It's just a meeting."

Leo drops into the armchair across from me, arms and legs sprawling as he relaxes. "Are you still stressing?"

"No."

"Fuck yes, he is." Thorin talks over me. The man is a bulldozer.

"Well knock it off," Leo demands, raising his glass and pointing it at me. "We haven't had a night off in weeks."

"It was worth it," I retort with a grin. Fuck working

for anyone else. Yeah, it took a metric shit-ton of work, but starting our own firm was the best idea we ever had.

"Debatable," Thorin mutters into his glass. "I'm so fucking pent up a stiff breeze could make me jizz."

Leo kicks Thor's foot. "You're just a class act tonight, huh?"

"All work and no play makes Thorin a horny boy," he growls, finishing his drink. "Christ, it's dead in here tonight."

I glance around at the lounge, every table occupied with people warming up for the night. "What are you talking about? It's packed."

"I dunno. I'm bored."

"You were horny five seconds ago, but now you're bored?" Leo laughs.

"I can be both." Thorin glowers at our partner over his glass of ice, his hard gray eyes just begging Leo to keep talking. But that's not Leo. He smirks and melts into his chair another twenty percent. I swear to Christ the man couldn't sit up straight to save his life. Not that it matters. He pulls it off and women fucking love it. I've seen more subs crawl into his lap than is fair.

Thorin tilts his head, looking at something behind me with a raised brow. I know that look. I don't even have to turn around. I lift my chin, getting Leo's attention. "Thorin spotted a bunny." Leo grins and turns to see. I don't bother. If it's what they want, I'm on board. As long as it's a chick, and she's into us, it'll do for tonight. So, I sip my drink and wait.

"Holy fuck," Leo murmurs.

Curiosity gets the better of me. I turn to look over the back of my chair. 'Holy fuck' is right. A woman moves through the crowd, tall and tan. She has to be at least 5'9" before she put those stilettos on. A black dress is plastered to her body like wet silk, the sheen reflecting the glow of the dim lights. It highlights the confident sway of her hips. Her hair is slicked back in a smooth, tight ponytail. It falls over her bare shoulder like a shimmering black rope.

She glances in our direction, eyes curious, but I sigh and sit back. That's some serious dom energy if I ever saw it. "Not a bunny, then," I say to Thorin, whose eyes are still locked on tall, dark, and man-eating. "You in the mood to get pegged? No judgment here, but I'm out."

"You think she's a top?" Leo asks skeptically.

"Obviously."

"You're wrong, Mal."

I raise my eyebrows at Leo. She's at least twenty feet away and isn't even looking this direction. Mr. Eye-Contact with his soul reading over here could give Miss Cleo a run for her money if he thinks he can tell which way her kinky pendulum swings. "Maybe she's a switch. Maybe. But that's not our bag either."

"You didn't look hard enough."

"I looked," I argue, finishing my drink and setting it on the table. What does it matter, anyway?

5

BRIELLE

This isn't you. The little voice niggles at the back of my brain, trying to get me to chicken out, but she can shut right up. I smooth my hands over the slick fabric of my dress. This is the power of good clothes. I feel, and look, like a complete badass, even if my inner wuss is trembling at the thought of what I'm planning.

"Just do it. Jump in. It's not that scary," I whisper to myself before straightening my shoulders and stepping through the doors of Club Sin. I have to sign in and acknowledge that I read and understand the rules. Oh, I read them alright. Especially the part about group play, but I'm not sure I have the lady stones for that.

I'm sent through to the lounge, and the sight sucks the oxygen right out of my body. A man—no, a god—stares me down as I walk to the bar. There are other people milling about, sitting at the bar, kissing, and teasing, but his eyes captivate me in a way I can't explain. He looks almost too big for the armchair he's lounging in. Sandy hair hangs in his eyes, long on top but shaved tight on the sides.

He's wearing expensive pants and a dress shirt, but the top buttons are undone, the cuffs rolled up. Tattoos cover his forearms and snake out from under his collar. If a Viking got sucked through a portal and landed in the middle of modern-day Chicago, he'd look like this.

He swirls the glass in his hand, an ice cube clinking against the glass, melting into his whiskey. The movement draws my gaze away from his, but only for a second. His gray eyes are steely and hard when I meet them again, but the unmistakable *lust* in his expression is what catches me off-guard. It feels strange that he's not disguising it. He doesn't look away or pretend he was looking at someone behind me.

No. His eyes meander down my body in a way that makes me think he could tear me apart while making me beg for more. He sips from his glass, and a shiver runs up my spine when I imagine kissing the last hint of whiskey from those lips.

Someone moves next to him, and when my gaze shifts, I wonder how in the hell I could have missed him. His eyes aren't hard at all. They widen as he takes me in, and his lips quirk up in a smirk that makes my heart backflip like it's trying to outdo Simone Biles. Holy god is he pretty.

A third man turns to peer at me over the top of his chair. His gaze is more… assessing. And whatever he sees, it's clearly not for him. He turns his back, but I can feel the other two watching me as I make my way to the bar. I order my drink and try to make my hands stop trembling when the bartender places it in front of me.

This was as far as my plan went. I don't know what I expected. It's not like I thought I was going to walk in and be dragged into an orgy the second my heel hit the carpet…. But I also may have underestimated how intimidating this would be.

When I turn around, martini in hand, the three men are gone and my heart sinks just a little. I should have brought a friend, but I don't have any friends besides Kelly, and something tells me this might not be her bag. I feel awkward standing by myself, so I go exploring.

No one stops me when I get to the elevator bank and press the button to call it. I know exactly where I want to go, what I want to try, even if I'm not entirely sure how to get it.

I get off on the fourth floor, giving my hands a shake. There are other rooms, but the one I want is at the far end of the hallway. Some of the doors are open, some closed, but as I pass each one, gasps and moans follow me, making my core clench and moisture coat my pussy. Maybe I should have worn panties…

The door to Room 30 is cracked, so I place my palm on it, and push it open. I don't see anyone as I venture inside. Dim light casts just enough illumination to set the mood, and when my eyes fall on the bundles of rope mounted on one wall, my heart stutters. One after another, in rainbow hues. I step up to bundles, running my fingers over one that's dyed a gorgeous shade of raspberry.

"Well, well…" a voice like dark chocolate and tobacco makes me jump, and I pull my hand back, fast as lightning. When I turn, I'm inches from a familiar face. The second man from the lounge stands before me. He's shed his jacket and rolled his sleeves up. Up close he's even more gorgeous than I realized in the lounge. Muscles ripple under his dark skin, and his green eyes are flecked with gold and black. I swallow hard, warmth rolling through me.

"Sorry, I—" I don't have an excuse, or really even a reason to apologize. But walking in here and touching things feels a little… intrusive.

"For what?" He grins, taking the rope off the wall and holding it out for me to take.

"I don't know," I laugh, gingerly taking the bundle and running my fingers over it. "I just didn't realize there was anyone else in here."

"You went straight for the rope, no wonder you didn't see us."

Us? Right on cue, I spot the two men in the corner, shadows and drapes partially obscuring them. The tattooed bad boy and the unimpressed suit from the lounge are watching us, their eyes unreadable. Something in my chest stutters, making each breath feel forced.

"Settle an argument for us, would you?" he says, running a thumb over his lip thoughtfully. "Are you a rigger, or a riggee?"

"Um…" Words have never failed me like this in all my life, but I can't think straight. He's so close I can see the individual strokes of the tattoos on his forearms. "Neither? I've never done this. *Any* of this."

His eyebrow jerks upward. "Shibari?"

"None of it. I've never done anything… kinky, unless you count a weak ass smack on the butt, which I don't."

Both of his eyebrows shoot up at that. "You're new to kink… and you joined Club Sin?"

"Yes," I say, feeling defensive. "Why the fuck does it matter? I don't need a reason to be here any more than you or your buddies."

"Oh, no. I didn't mean it like that." His tone is sincere,

so I try to lock down the frustration of being questioned before I even get to experience the things I came here for.

"It's just not how people usually end up here. You're diving into the deep end on your first day of swimming lessons. It's ballsy, and I can absolutely appreciate that. I'm Leo." He holds out his hand, waiting for me to shake it. I switch the rope to my left hand and place my palm in his.

"Bree," I reply. He repeats my name, letting it roll off of his tongue like something he likes the taste of.

"Well, Bree, if you're curious, we can show you a bit. With your consent, of course." Those green eyes search mine like he's looking for something specific. Or maybe he's just really into eye contact.

My heart races. It *screams* for me to say yes. *Show me everything!* I try to keep my poker face, try to get my frantically pounding pulse to ease up. His grin widens as he watches my face. Despite my best efforts, he looks at me like he sees right through my skin to the secrets I've never told a soul.

"You want to tie me up…?"

"Absolutely I do." His answer catches me by surprise. I don't know why I thought people would be secretive or subtle here. Why would they be? This is one of very few places where none of us have to hide what we want. "But if you're not sure, why don't you watch the three of us, and then you can decide?"

The three of them… a shiver shoots up my spine at the thought. Three sets of hands, all those fingers dragging over my skin… For a moment I lose myself, my thoughts consumed by the idea. Three men. Three gorgeous men. Over me, under me, inside of me… but then I realize I'm the interloper here. "Oh, Jesus. I'm so sorry." I say, backing toward the door. "I didn't mean to walk in on your session or anything."

"Stop."

The voice is smokey, deep and rough. The command is unmistakably meant for me. I freeze, my heels superglued to the floor, my eyes finding the tattooed Viking. My chest rises and falls with each shallow breath. He steps out of the corner and prowls toward me like a tiger, his intense eyes locked on mine, as if daring me to look away.

He glances over his shoulder at the man in the suit. "Told you so," his voice vibrates through the air, making me wonder what he told him. Something about me? Can't be, considering we've never spoken before this moment. But then his focus, and all of its raw, spine-tingling power, settles back on me and I find that I don't really care.

"You're not interrupting. You are *very* welcome, regardless of participation." Oh, God. I *really* should have worn those panties, but I'm not arguing with him if he says I can stay and watch. I wanted to play tonight, but maybe it's best if I just watch so I don't fuck up in the future.

"Okay," I say, trying to force the breathy quality out of my voice, but it's impossible when I can't seem to catch my breath. I glance at the man in the suit. He still hasn't said anything. He's… observing, his head tilted to the side, eyes tightening as he frowns at me thoughtfully.

He crooks a finger in my direction, beckoning me closer. I move on instinct, floating to stand in front of him without even thinking about it. He's a towering, imposing figure in that suit, and I can't help but think that's how he likes to be seen. Lifting my chin I stare back into his eyes, refusing to back down just because he's big and scary.

His lips quirk, fighting a smile. "You're a troublemaker, aren't you?" he murmurs quietly.

"No." I say archly. "You can't be a troublemaker if you don't get caught."

"Spoken like a true brat." His chuckle catches me by surprise. "I'm Mal, that ugly fucker is Thorin." He gestures at the dangerously handsome tattoo guy who rolls his eyes.

"Don't listen to him. That tie is just limiting the amount of oxygen that gets to his big head." Thorin grins broadly, taking the rope from my hands. "Alright boys, who's the willing victim?" Mal shakes his head, but Leo raises his hand.

Thorin calls Mal a pussy, getting an eye roll in return. Leo yanks his shirt off, and my mouth goes dry. "You're going to need another rope," he says to Thorin, but his eyes are fixed on me. "I'm a lot thicker than little Bree here." Thicker is… accurate. Walking slab of muscle would also be accurate.

It's not that I'm a delicate little waif. The patriarchal society can pry my ice cream from my cold dead fingers. I'm not giving that up just to fit in a smaller size. I work out, but that's really about stress relief. Well, stress relief and a way to exorcize some of my pent-up sexual frustration.

At five foot nine, I'm tall for a woman, and wearing heels, I'm often taller than half the men in the room. Just not in *this* room. These three tower over me like imposing sex gods. Tall and *thick*.

"Hands by your side," Thorin directs Leo, who plays along despite looking less than amused. Thorin situates the rope behind Leo's head, draping it over his shoulders. I watch his hands move, mesmerized. He makes it look so easy, but it's clear this is a skill he's developed. Each knot is carefully placed, the tension set at just the right level.

He weaves the tail ends, knotting and adjusting until

ROOM THIRTY

he has Leo's hands cuffed by his sides. His arms are pinned in place by the intricate harness that hugs his torso. There isn't enough air in the room to keep my lungs inflating properly.

"Hot, huh?" Thorin grins deviously. I nod. This was a pipe dream. Something I never really thought I'd get to try. But I'm here, this is real, and I know exactly what I want.

6

THORIN

I fucking told him so. Bree might have walked into Club Sin like a dominatrix, but Mal definitely jumped to the wrong conclusion. I feel her eyes following my hands as I rig up Leo. It's a speedy chest harness with cuffs, nothing crazy, but Bree's gaze is hooded, her lips parted. Her breathing is rapid. Shallow. Excited.

"That's amazing," she murmurs, her focus still fixed on the rope. "Can—?" she pauses and clears her throat.

"You wanna try?" I ask. "I can show you a couple safe, simple ties, but you should really take a course if you want to be a rigger. There are nerves and pressure points to watch out for, basic knot tying, safety…" I watch her out of the corner of my eye, and start untying Leo. He's a willing demonstrator, but being tied up isn't his bag.

Bree is being cagey. I can feel it. Maybe she just needs a push to speak up. Leo and Mal study her face too, and when Bree's nose wrinkles subtly, I can't help smirking at Mal. *Motherfucking told you so!* He shrugs, admitting defeat but not looking too disappointed about being wrong.

"I don't know about rigger classes, I…" she trails off, chewing her lip and then soothing it with her tongue. "You know what?" She raises her voice suddenly, the airy quality replaced with something far more fierce. "I've done my research. I know how to negotiate. I understand safe words and rope safety. I've watched every single video on Shibari that I could track down. Fuck, I even took an online course. I joined Club Sin for exactly one reason." She points at Leo, the coil of rope loose on his chest as I finish freeing him. "I want that."

"You want me?" Leo chuckles and lets his eyes drift over her body, making a scene out of appreciating her curves. "Baby, you can have me any day of the week, and twice on Sunday." Mal rolls his eyes, but Bree tucks her bottom lip between her teeth, suppressing a grin.

"You want someone to tie you up. Take control?" It's one of the first things Mal has really said to her, and she reacts like she's seeing him for the first time, surprise and fascination lighting up her eyes. "You want the friction of the rope against your skin, something to fight against while you get fucked?"

"Yes." Bree says the word on a hard exhale. It looks like it's costing her to say that out loud, but she lifts her chin and straightens her spine, reclaiming that badass attitude we saw in the bar. My dick has been at half-mast just watching her, but that—fuck me. I like my women strong. Submission means nothing to me if they don't have a backbone to begin with.

"The three of us come as a set. We like sharing our pets, but that's probably a bit much for you. We can find you an easier dom to start with." Leo's eyes flash in my direction, pissed that I'd even offer that. But I'm on to her now. Nothing makes a bratty rope bunny braver than being told they can't handle something. I can see it in the way Bree levels that gorgeous gaze at me. *Challenge accepted…*

"You're already underestimating me," she says archly. "I think I can manage three little boys."

I chuckle and rub my thumb over my lower lip. "Three little boys. Ouch." I give her a wounded expression and glance at Mal and Leo. At six foot two, I'm the shortest of the three of us. Mal is built like a fucking tank in a suit. Leo hasn't skipped a gym day in the five years I've known him, and he's hung like a fucking horse. It's safe to say none of our egos are bruised, and there's no hiding how much they liked her answer.

"Alright, let's sort out details." I rub my hands together, slowly. I love negotiations. I know it's something most people just want to get through, but something about having a sub say what they want out loud makes me harder than fucking granite; doubly hard when they do it with mouthy bravado like little Bree.

Mal pulls a notebook out of my bag. Keeping track of things is his specialty, to the point that I'm kind of surprised he hasn't tried to make a spreadsheet for this yet. Actually, I don't know for certain that he hasn't. It would be very on brand for my stepbrother.

"Are you okay with someone walking in here and watching? It happens sometimes." Bree's eyes flare, and she nods without hesitating. Interesting…

"We're a package deal, and we don't switch. Our bunnies don't get a turn at tying us up, you okay with that?"

"God, yes."

"Are you going to be a gentle bunny and obey right away?" I want to laugh when her eye twitches. "I'll take that as a no. Do you enjoy being physically overpowered? Forced to submit when you're naughty?"

"Yes, and yes." Again, no hesitation.

"Any allergies or medical conditions we should be aware of, physical or mental?"

"Does being Type A count?" Bree asks with a grin.

"No." Mal's voice catches her attention, and she turns that grin on him.

"Then no."

"Fun part," I say, giving her ponytail a little yank, just enough to get her attention. "Stop me when I get to something you're uncomfortable with performing or having performed on you. Masturbation — fellatio — cunnilingus — rimming — fingering — vaginal penetration — anal penetration with fingers, tongues, or toys," I leave a long pause between each act, but she doesn't even flinch. "Anal sex — sex toys, including vibrators, dildos, butt plugs, anal beads. Choking?" Still not so much as a hint of discomfort.

"You really haven't played with kink at all? And you're okay with all of this?" Leo's eyebrows are sky high.

Bree nods, her cheeks turning pink. "I haven't done anything kinky with other people... but on my own, I've experimented a bit." She says it with a little shrug, clearly unaware that the three of us are running through infinite, and very creative mental images of her polishing her pearl.

"And...? What do you like?" Mal asks, a brow rising along with the corner of his mouth.

Bree bites her lip, her answer whooshing out of her. "Butt plugs, vibrators, obviously, dildos, nipple play, and... double penetration." Her voice squeaks when she makes that last admission, but my dick doesn't care. It swells against the front of my pants, aching and dripping. Fuck, she's sexy.

"Dirty girl," Leo says, his face lit up like it's Christmas morning. I probably have the same expression on my face. Either this woman is too good to be true, or we hit the fucking lottery tonight.

I go on with a grin. "Acceptable bondage: hands tied behind or in front — wrists to ankles — spreader bars —"

"Ooh, yes please," Bree breathes excitedly.

"Noted," Mal chips in, a great big grin flashing across his normally serious face. He's what you might call a *fan* of spreader bars. The playroom in the house we share has a set in every size and configuration you can put your mind to, courtesy of Mallon's obsession with easy access.

"Tied to furniture — blindfolds — gags — rope — handcuffs, metal or leather — tape?"

Bree grins at me. "Yes, please."

"Okay," I chuckle. "I won't do suspension with a first timer, so we don't even need to go into that unless we choose to play again… Let's talk pain. None of us are serious sadists, but if a bunny likes pain, we're happy to dole it out." Leo tosses a wink in her direction. We all have our bag, and the flogger is his.

"I have a high pain tolerance," Bree offers confidently. "And I like it in solo play, but I've never had anyone… participate."

"Alright, stop me when I get to something you don't want or something you're really interested in. Spanking — paddling — flogging —"

"I want all of that," she interjects, and Mal jots it down. Behind our enthusiastic little bunny, he shakes his head with a grin. Mal hates to be wrong, but from the look on his face, he's okay being mistaken just this once.

7

BRIELLE

My mouth has written *a lot* of checks tonight. But with the exception of bodily fluids and knife play, nothing Thorin has listed is that shocking. I didn't agree to anything I haven't fantasized about or tried on my own. Still… three men. That prudish little voice in my head taunts me. *Really? You reaaaally think you can handle all that? Just because you tried two skinny dildos at once, doesn't make you Queen of Cock-Taking.*

Mal, the big guy still wearing the suit, writes everything down. I peek at him over my shoulder, appreciating his broad shoulders and the exquisite tailoring of his suit coat around his biceps. He's handsome, but it's understated somehow. Like, his individual features aren't exceptional. Square jaw, full lips, dark eyes. But the package is more than the parts. He's expressive in a way that's hard to ignore.

And then the contract is done. The negotiations settled. Mal sets the notes aside and eyes me like I'm a puzzle to be sorted out. Thorin stretches his neck from side to side, his eyes bright with focused excitement. "Are you ready? Or would you rather get some water or a snack first?"

I giggle nervously and it's such an uncharacteristic sound for me to make that it almost doesn't even register that it came from me. "Sorry, I'm nervous…" I pause and clear my throat. If I leave now, I'm not sure the chances of me coming back are very high. I want this so badly — have wanted it for as long as I can remember — and the idea of walking away now feels like self-betrayal.

"I'm ready now." *Am I, though?* I'm about to hand my body over to complete strangers, and we haven't even kissed. Negotiating felt more like a business transaction than foreplay, but, for me, that actually lowered the intimidation factor. Business I get, and removing myself emotionally makes it a whole lot easier to be honest. If I'm not talking about *me,* I can say anything out loud.

Yes, that woman wants to be choked. Is she comfortable deep-throating? Absolutely. Praise kink? Hell, yes. Degradation? Bring it on.

Thorin grins as Leo steps toward me, running a hand up my arm, fingers brushing over my skin. He leans down, his lips brushing the shell of my ear. My core clenches and the hairs on the back of my neck prickle, diffusing into a full body buzz when he whispers. "Don't be nervous. We'll take care of you." There's a teasing edge to his words that doesn't exactly make me less jittery. If anything, it makes anticipation spiral up around me like a cocoon of adrenaline.

A wall presses at me from behind, but then I realize it's not a wall. It's a rock-hard slab of muscle hiding behind an expensive suit. A strong arm wraps around my shoulder, the hand gripping the column of my throat, forcing my chin up. My head falls back on Mal's shoulder, the position arching my back. I close my eyes, relaxing against him with a purposefully controlled breath.

"So pretty," he growls in my ear, a hand squeezing my breast roughly. My skin hums with barely contained electricity as Leo captures my mouth with his. It's not the kind of first kiss I'm used to. He doesn't brush his lips over mine. He doesn't hesitate or test the proverbial waters. He *takes*. His tongue plunges between my lips, possessive and hard. He growls in the back of his throat, and that one little sound makes my heartbeat pound triple-time.

Unseen fingers find the zipper at my side, inching it down with rasping clicks. Mal takes advantage of the loosened bodice, a rough hand slipping underneath. His fingers roll my nipple, plucking at it until it's hard and tight, the ache pouring through my body.

The unmistakable sound of rope whips through the air, making my breath hitch. I can't see Thorin, but I'm pretty sure I have an idea of what he's up to. Mal turns us, and there's the sexy-as-fuck Viking. He cracks his neck, and glances over at me with dark promise in his eyes as he unbundles a length of rope. I shift my weight from one foot to the other, pressing my thighs together. "Someone's excited…" Mal's voice purrs in my ear. He flexes those fingers on my throat, possessively holding me closer. A soft moan vibrates in my throat on every exhale, the ache growing inside me already begging to be eased.

"Tell me your safe word, Pet. Show me you know how to use it." Leo nips at my earlobe, hard enough to make me gasp, but the pain warms, rippling down my neck.

"R-red," I pant.

"Such a good girl," he murmurs, and I preen at the praise. Maybe it's because I never go looking for external validation, but oh god, the way he says it sends shivers racing down my spine. He kneels, unfastening the straps around each of my ankles. He lifts my feet one at a time, and gently slips my heels off. "You won't be needing those," he says, winking at me as he stands again.

Leo's heavy hands slide my dress down my shoulders to hang at my waist. Cool air teases my breasts. I reach up to cover myself, but Mal tuts, pulling my arms behind my body. He loops a forearm under my elbows, lifting my arms behind me and trapping them between us with ease.

"Don't you dare hide from us, Pet," he growls in a rough reprimand, his free hand circling my throat. Leo watches, his expression avid.

I'm physically helpless in under a second, my heart racing. It's not that I'm trying to get away. Not at all. I'm just not used to men who don't treat me like I'm made of paper-thin glass and dandelion fluff. The reality finally hits: I'm going to get *exactly* what I came here for.

It sinks in, and the realization is such a fucking relief. The deep-seated fear and shame that I've carried for so long melts away. Those quiet internal whispers that always made me feel like I'm somehow… *wrong*. Abnormal. A freak. Those whispers take a hike, chased away by men who not only don't bat a lash at my fantasies, but welcome the chance to fulfill them. Enthusiastically.

I can't look away as Leo lowers his mouth to my nipple, eyes locked on mine. He draws my entire areola between his lips in a hot, wet, open-mouthed kiss before dragging his teeth over the buzzing peak.

"Look at her squirm," Mal chuckles, his lips buried in my hair. "She can't press those thighs together hard enough. Give her a bite, Leo."

A smug expression flashes through Leo's eyes as he gazes up at me. The suckling of his tongue dancing over that tight little bundle of nerves is enough to make me weak in the knees, but when he bites down, increasing the pressure and baring his teeth, my legs just about give out.

Holy shit. I might be in over my head, but I have *never* felt this good. I arch harder against Mal's steel hold, trying to push my breasts closer to Leo's mouth, but neither of them seems willing to give me more, no matter how hard I try to push it.

Mal brushes feathery kisses along my ear. "Such a greedy pet. You can't get enough of his mouth, can you?"

"No…" I moan, and I really can't. Every flick of his tongue, every nip and scrape, is heaven renewed, over and over again. But Leo pulls back and aims a short smack at my nipple, making me gasp as the intensity roils through my bloodstream.

"No, *what?*" Leo's eyes go hard. "You said you know what you're doing here. Is that how you talk to a dom?"

"No, sir," I cry out. My core trembles, and I flush as I feel a drip of arousal roll down my thigh. I can't turn to see Mal's face, but I do my best. "No, sir. I can't get enough. I want his mouth everywhere. I'm a greedy pet."

"Yes, you are." Leo smirks and grabs the dress, still bunched at my waist, shimmying it the rest of the way down my hips. It falls to a puddle of liquid silk on the floor around my feet, and when I peek down at him, he's on his knees, and the dark lust in his expression takes the breath right out of my lungs.

I am so, *so* glad I skipped the panties.

8

LEO

My knees hit the mat as Bree's dress falls around her feet. "Fuck," I growl. She stares down at me, tits heaving with each breath she takes, straining against Mallon's hold. Her ass thrusts back against his hips and from the pained expression on his face, she's giving him quite the lap dance. I'd be jealous, but the sight in front of me is enough to wipe my mind to a blank slate.

Carefully trimmed curls adorn her pubic bone, silky soft and as dark as her ponytail. I run a single finger over them, trailing down to the glistening arousal coating her luscious thighs. "Fuck, that's a pretty pussy." I tear my gaze away from heaven, and look behind her at Mal. "She's so fucking wet. Dirty girl was wandering around the club with her pussy dripping down her thighs."

I hear a rumbling growl from Thorin, but his hands are full of his rope. Behind Bree, Mal closes his eyes, doing his best not to jizz in his pants, most likely. But when he speaks, his voice doesn't carry a hint of that struggle. Dude has a serious dom voice when he wants to. "Get a fucking taste, then. Show her what happens to dirty girls who forget their panties."

He sure as fuck isn't in charge of me, and there's a snowflake's chance in hell of me calling him 'sir.' Three doms with one sub might be a tall order for most, but for three doms with a serious voyeur streak, and the ability to check our egos at the door, this is what works for us. And judging by the way Bree clamps her thighs together, rubbing them for any ounce of relief she can get, it works for her, too.

"Spread your legs, Bree." I keep my voice low, making her work to hear me. Mallon is the growler, not me. I prefer to speak softly and swing a big dick, a phrase both Thorin and Mal roll their eyes at, but subs don't seem to mind. Especially the big dick part.

She bites her lower lip and does as she's told, but her feet only move a couple of inches. I press my middle finger to her pussy, slipping just the first knuckle inside her before pulling back out. Bree moans pitifully, but I land a sharp smack on the inside of her thigh and get to my feet, leaning over her.

Mal releases his hold on her throat, but keeps her arms pinned behind her back. I grip her jaw, forcing her eyes up; pushing the edge of rough to make my point. "I told you to spread your legs. You only spread them an inch, so that's all you get in that greedy little pussy. You want my fingers? You want my tongue?"

Bree nods frantically, her gorgeous brown eyes wide. I raise my eyebrows, but she doesn't say it, so I land a quick slap to her pussy. Not hard enough to hurt, just enough to shock her. But from the way those eyes flare with excitement before melting back into heavy-lidded lust, she fucking liked that way too much. Well, not *too* much. It's never *too* much.

"Yes, sir," she breathes.

"Good girl." I tap her feet with one of mine. "Spread." Bree does as she's told, her legs parting so quickly that Mal has to support her weight until her toes settle back on the mat. I kneel in front of her, a filthy parishioner, eager to worship. Mal fists her hair, angling her face down toward me.

"Watch him eat that dripping cunt," he growls in her ear. The muscles in her stomach tense as she stares at me. I bring the tip of my tongue to her clit, feathering little flicks against the bundle of nerves but never giving her any real pressure. I tongue every fold, circling the hood of her clit. Bree peers down at me, eyes rapt and glazed with lust. She licks her lips, but they remain parted in a soft, awe-filled pout.

"I bet she tastes good," Mal mutters at me. I pull her clit between my lips and hum in agreement. We all have our kinks, and Mallon gets hard making them squirm with his voice. I've watched him talk a sub ninety-nine percent of the way to an orgasm, and from the way Bree's hips keep bucking, she's a fan of his brand of dirty talk. She's going to be a fun one to restrain, I can already tell she's going to fight and wriggle, beg and plead.

Still, eating a writhing pussy is hard work. I grab handfuls of her ass, yanking her hips back to my face so I can bury my tongue in her cunt. My nose bumps her clit, already swollen and peeking out of its hood. I shake my head from side to side and Bree cries out, half-moan, half-scream and a gush of sweetness hits my tongue.

I pull back, letting her watch me as I wipe the moisture from my chin and suck it off. Looking over her shoulder at Mal, I grin. "We've got a gusher." Mal groans and holds her steady. I turn my gaze to Bree. "Wait until he gets his hands on this pussy. You're going to need to hydrate." Her pupils flare, and even in the soft light of the Shibari studio, there is no disguising her excitement.

9

THORIN

I'm trying to focus on the rope; set up the scene in my head, but Mal and Leo have our little bunny moaning and whimpering just a couple feet away. Mal is whispering dirty shit in her ear, just loud enough to distract me, while Leo eats the fuck out of her pussy. The skin of Bree's chest and neck are flushed, and she looks about 30 seconds from melting into a puddle of liquid sex. Every time I glance over, that flush has spread further, and she looks more and more shaky.

Mal's mouth is just a *parade* of filth. "Look at him eat that pretty pussy… dude, give her a couple fingers, I bet she's aching for it…" A gasp and more moans. "Thank your dom for licking that pussy." I can hold my own in the dirty talk arena, but I have to admit, he has a way of making subs melt.

"Th—thank you. Thank you for licking my pussy, sir."

"Don't let her come," I warn loudly, rubbing my palm over the hard-on ready to rip my pants to shreds. Christ, she's going to be hell on my control. I train my eyes on the richly dyed set of teal hemp rope I brought out of my bag.

The stuff at the club is fine, but mine is better. I have a process for breaking it in and sanitizing it. I wind the last length around my bicep and fist, carefully setting it next to the longer ones. It's good to have a variety.

Another gasp and a desperate whimper. "Seriously, Leo. Edge her all you want, but don't let our pet come. I want to take my time with her and don't want her all boneless. Yet."

Bree makes a whining sound in her throat as Leo abandons her pussy and turns to grin at me, his face wet with her arousal. "You sure? She's all juicy. I can just clean this up for you…"

I scowl at him. Fucking antagonist. "Leave it. She can drip and beg just as well in rope."

Leo chuckles and jumps to his feet. Mal uses his grip on Bree's hair to tilt her head to the side. He presses kisses along the slope of her shoulder and licks the curve of her neck before biting the pressure point above her collar bone. She watches Leo and I, eyes only half-focused as she shivers and melts against Mal like soft butter. Her velvety eyes find mine as I pick up the longest length of rope.

"Alright, boys. Any requests?" I swing the tail of the rope lazily and let my gaze wander over Bree lasciviously.

"Dress," Leo offers.

Mal grunts out, "Crab tie," at the same time. I could have called those answers a mile away. Mal likes them helpless; Leo likes them on display.

"Both it is then," I reply, raising my eyebrows as I grab the half-way point of the teal rope, giving it a little snap. I like it all.

Bree jumps, pressing her thighs together. I step toward her slowly, drawing out every movement for her greedy gaze. Behind the obvious lust, there's a fascination in her expression that I can't get over. It might just be the novelty of living out a fantasy, but I don't think so. I recognize that spark of realization, of fulfillment, at finding the thing you've always been missing. At least, I think I recognize it in her eyes, but what the fuck do I know?

Mallon releases her hair and arms but stays close behind to support her. The last thing we need is for her to go all wobbly and fall face first on the mat. I step right into her personal space, forcing her to lift her chin to meet my eye, which she does without hesitation, her lips parted.

I grip her cheeks with my free hand, fingers right under her cheekbones. Lowering my face so close our noses brush, I make my voice hard. "Keep looking at me with that pretty mouth open, and I'll find something to fill it up with." Under my fingers, her jaw moves. But she's not an obedient little bunny. I chuckle as her mouth opens wide, challenge flashing in her irises.

Some tops like subs to crawl, avert their gaze, and submit like little dolls. Not me. I love the fire in her eyes. I like to work for it. "Leo," I drawl, grinning at him over my shoulder. "Be a dear and get a gag out of my bag."

"Which one?"

"Dealer's choice. Just pick something I can hear her moan through."

Leo smirks and opens a pocket in my travel bag, unrolling my collection. He drags his finger over them one by one. I'm still holding her face, but turn it so she can watch him pick out her jewelry. He brings a white leather one, with a small, white silicone bit.

"Someone is feeling generous. Look at that bitty thing," I mutter grumpily, but really, this one is perfect for a newbie. "Leo is being soft on you."

Leo flips me the bird and hands the gag to Mal, who

pops it across her mouth and fastens it around her head wordlessly. Bree peers up at me through her lashes, her expression almost smug. "Don't worry, we'll get something in there later to really stretch that pretty mouth," I growl.

I slip the loop of rope around the back of her neck and use it to pull her naked body against mine. "Let's hear that safe word, Pet."

"Red." The word comes out of her mouth thick around the gag, but it's perfectly discernible.

"Good girl." I don't break eye contact as I tie the column of knots down her front. Below her collarbone, just under her breasts, above and below her belly button. Her breathing shallows as I move lower, her pulse racing under the delicate skin of her neck. Mal sees it too, and smirks as he lowers his mouth to lick the throbbing pulse point.

I carefully measure the placement of the last knot, slipping my fingers into her sopping pussy and rubbing her swollen little clit. "Fuck," I say to Leo. "You weren't kidding." Her lips are wet, the moisture coating her thighs. I squat down, running the rope between her legs and situating that knot exactly where I want it. Air hisses through Bree's teeth as I stand, pulling the tails around the thick globes of her ass. I have zero doubt that my little knot is hitting the spot when her knees go weak, and Mal has to grab her to hold her steady.

The rope trails up her back, looping around the back of her neck. I weave them forward and back, drawing the rope snug to form diamonds down her front and bands of rope that hug her hips, waist, tits, and chest. I tie off the ends, weaving them down her spine.

If I were feeling cruel and she were more experienced, I'd suspend her from that handle and let her try to get off against her little happy knot. But I don't want to push her too far. Not until I've tested her green list. She said yes to, or straight up asked for, plenty to keep us occupied and entertained for hours. Days. Hell, maybe weeks.

I smooth my fingers along each section of rope, making sure nothing is pinching or twisted. I watch the way her face relaxes and her breathing settles as my fingers run underneath the rope, knuckles grazing her nipples.

Every breath she takes makes the knot shift against her clit. She lets out a full body shiver and then gasps when the rope works double-time. I glance at Mal, who wordlessly reassures me that he has a solid hold on her, before I take a step back to admire her. Christ, she's beautiful.

Behind me, Leo shucks his pants, the buckle hitting the floor with a muffled clink. Bree watches him with hungry eyes. I turn to see what has captivated her attention so fully, and find him with his dick in hand, stroking it for her.

"He's got a big dick, doesn't he?" I ask her with a chuckle. Bree nods, not looking away for a second as she wets her lips. That one little lick sets my already-aching dick into aching territory. Leo squeezes hard, a drop of pre-cum shining at the tip. I'm not into dudes, not enough to fuck them at least, but I sure as hell appreciate her reaction to it.

Mal leans over her shoulder and bites her earlobe before whispering, "He's going to fuck you with that thing. Stretch your tight little pussy around it while I fuck this pretty asshole." His hand moves between them, hidden from view, but judging by the way Bree sucks a breath and arches her back, I'd say he found his target. Her eyelids flutter, her eyes rolling back in her head.

"You want that, don't you?" Mal gives her harness a tug, driving the knot against her clit.

"Yes, sir," she moans around the gag. A drip of drool pools at her lower lip, and Leo steps closer, wiping it away with his fingers. It's almost a sweet moment, but Leo grabs her cheeks and sticks two fingers in her mouth, demanding she suck them around the gag. He fucks her mouth with them until she has them good and wet, then he lowers his hand and uses her spit to lube up his cock. Bree's eyes water but she doesn't lose a shred of that insanely hot enthusiasm. If anything, Mal is having to hold her back.

"Walk over to the platform. Turn and sit down," I demand, pointing at a large, round, cushioned platform in the middle of the room. Club Sin keeps washable waterproof covers for their custom furniture. At least for the things that are likely to get wet, and if we do this right, our little bunny is going to make a mess.

10

BRIELLE

My head is swimming, lust coloring every emotion and thought until it's overwhelming. Thorin's rope "dress" makes me feel more exposed than if I were nude. It hugs my body, snug, but not painful. The mirrors around the room give me glimpses of the dark teal diamonds highlighting my torso. It's better than I ever imagined. I can barely tear my eyes away from my reflection. The rope squeezes my skin, forming a web perfectly designed to put me on display. It lifts my breasts, nips in at my waist, highlights my hips, and disappears between my legs…

Jesus Christ. Whatever he did down there is straight sin. Delicious sin. A bump—a knot, from the feel of it—slips between my labia, bumping the underside of my clit with every breath I take. I can barely move without a jolt of pleasure threatening to take me to my knees, and this mad man wants me to walk all the way to the huge round bed. Ten feet. I could literally cartwheel that distance under normal circumstances. But trussed up like this… I dunno. Can orgasms kill?

"You heard him," Mal rumbles from behind my right ear. He uses his grip on the rope woven over my spine to push me a step toward the bed. The knot hits just right, dragging a gasping moan out of my body.

"Oh, fuck," I mutter, struggling to keep my eyes from slamming shut. When I open them, Thorin has stripped out of his clothes like Houdini starring in a strip show. His dick bobs in front of him, just as long as Leo's, though maybe not as thick. What really grabs my attention though, is the path of silver beads that run along the underside. Thorin gives me a knowing grin, stroking the length of his erection and pulling it toward his stomach so the light catches on the balls. Pairs of smaller beads run up the entire length, with larger ones at the tip.

Leo tuts like a disappointed schoolteacher. "Such language from our little bunny." He reaches back into their bag of tricks, pulling out a black, phallic handle attached to hundreds of tiny leather strands. My heart pounds as I watch him swish it in the air, shaking the strands so they all hang down like a horse's tail. Mal forces me to take another step, sending a hard wave of pleasure out through my body.

Leo circles behind us, and I feel Mal release the rope. Breath warms my shoulder — Leo's breath. "If you're going to swear at your doms and drag your feet when you're told to move, you're going to have a hard time sitting down tomorrow."

Soft leather tails caress my backside. He drags them over my skin, and holy hell, does it feel… nice. It's gentle, almost ticklish. But then there's a soft whoosh as he takes it away and a split second later a sharp spank ignites my skin. The slap of palm meeting flesh cuts through the room like staccato thunder, echoing in my ears. The sensation morphs from a hard sting to an electric heat that sizzles my nerves. Leo grabs the burning spot roughly, jiggling my ass.

"Put your hands behind your head. Spread your legs."

I refrain from asking if he's going to arrest me as I wiggle my feet outward gingerly. Something tells me I'm already in for it. Another sharp crack lands on my ass, stinging the other cheek. I squeal and lift up on my toes, but the heat is already spreading, transforming the pain into hard pleasure. Leather tails tickle the heated skin of my backside, swishing back and forth, swinging away and landing on my ass.

The licks get harder, faster, not pain exactly, but a burning heat that thuds through my flesh, lighting my blood on fire. Leo turns me to face Thorin and pushes my shoulders forward, bending me at a 90-degree angle. Mal holds my chin, forcing me to look forward. Thorin eyes me with a smirk, rubbing a palm over his cock as he arranges bundles of deep teal rope.

The flogger kisses the backs of my thighs before landing with a deep sting. Leo whirls it, sharp rapid smacks cover my butt cheeks. My pussy flutters with every fall of those leather tails. My brain goes foggy, my body floating away.

Warm breath tickles my neck. "Every time you sit down on this sweet little ass tomorrow, you're going to remember what happens to naughty pets." Leo's voice is pure sex; seductive and velvety. "Now move."

It's all he needs to say. I can feel all three of them watching me as I take careful steps. The knot still bumps my clit with every movement, making my core clench futilely for relief. I make it to the bed, arousal dripping down my legs, and sit gingerly, another gasp hissing through my teeth. I pull my lips between my teeth and resist the urge to rock against the knot. I'm sure I'll be punished if I do, which honestly makes it all the more tempting.

All three of them step close, towering over me. Thorin and Leo cross their arms as Mal unbuttons his shirt. He lets it hang open, going for his belt, eyes fixed on me. They're all watching me like I'm something to be devoured. From the shared expression on their faces, it's clear I haven't seen anything yet.

Thorin stoops to pick up two smaller lengths of rope. He sets one on the bed, next to my hip, holding the other in his hand. Leo circles behind me as Mal sheds his pants, kicking them aside. They move as a unit, exchanging subtle glances and gestures. Thorin lifts his chin and, a second later, strong hands hook under my arms, yanking me back on the bed.

Leo scoots right up behind me, that huge dick of his trapped between us, gliding along my spine. His thick thighs bracket my hips as he palms my belly possessively, making sure there isn't a nanometer of room between my ass and him.

Lips caress my shoulder. Hot skin presses against my back as Leo reaches around me with both arms. He grips my knees, pulling them up toward my chest. My thighs are spread wide as he plants my heels on the bed.

I'm exposed. Utterly and completely exposed. Cool air hits my pussy, and I am painfully aware of the moisture dripping out of me. Thorin runs his thumb over his lower lip, eyes fixed in dark desire at my sex.

"That is a *pretty* pussy," he mutters appreciatively. I blush, strangely pleased by his approval.

Mal, finally naked, tosses a bottle of something to Leo,

who snatches it out of the air with one hand. I get an eyeful of his erection as he strolls toward us so casually, I could swear he was out for a Sunday picnic. His dick has zero chill though. It juts toward me, so hard and swollen that the taught skin is shiny. The head is almost bulbous and flares out to a pronounced ridge at the base of the glans. The ache in my lower belly turns into a firestorm when I imagine that thing pounding my g-spot.

Leo drips liquid over my shoulders and down my back, sending a shiver of excitement through me. He reaches around, and glistening trails of oil race down my breasts and stomach, pooling where the rope squeezes my flesh. He drizzles my thighs and calves before snapping the bottle shut.

And then hands are everywhere. Mal and Thorin each claim a leg, dragging nails over my skin and massaging my calves. They are not delicate. Fingertips knead my muscles, targeting tight spots and working them hard. Leo's hands work the oil over my body, skimming the tender skin under my breasts in a loving caress before pinching my nipples hard enough to make me cry out.

"Grab those ankles," Leo demands in a low rumble. I do as he says, even though it makes my clit grind against the rope and stars flash in my vision. I rock against it again; anything for a smidge of relief, but Leo catches me. He palms my belly, fingers hooking in the rope. He gives it a tug, and I let out a keening cry.

It hurts so good. Soooo, so good. The instant of pain turns into a full body shiver; a tiny taste of ecstasy that makes my soul hum. My head swims, my body relaxing. This is so much better than I could have ever hoped for.

"Did I say you could rub your cunt on our rope?" he growls.

I shake my head and say "No, sir," as best I can with the gag still pulling at my lips.

"That's right. You get pleasure when *we* say you get pleasure. If you're going to be a greedy little whore, you're going to get a lot more than one spank."

Leo's open hand lands with a slap over my pussy. I moan against my gag, my head falling back on his shoulder. I'm trying not to wiggle, but the dirtier his mouth gets and the rougher he is with me, the more I can't bear to hold still. My entire body throbs with white-hot need.

A need that doesn't ease up when Thorin positions my forearm alongside my calf and starts weaving and knotting an intricate web, binding my arm against my leg. He repeats the ties on my other side. Leo murmurs in my ear, telling me what a good girl I am as he pets my outer labia, lighting up nerve endings but avoiding anything that would actually help me come.

I'm so frustrated and distracted by him, that it takes me a second to realize that Thorin and Mal have stepped back to admire my predicament. I'm not just vulnerable bound up like this. I'm helpless. Exposed. I fucking love it.

"Do you know what that's called?" Thorin asks. I shake my head. I've probably seen it, but I can barely put two words together, let alone recall a specific tie. "That's a crab tie," he says with a devious grin. "Any guesses on why we like it?" I shake my head again. I could take some shots at it, but at this point, I'd rather he says it.

"The beauty of the crab tie is positioning. Leo over there can put you pretty much anywhere he wants, but no matter where we put you, your mouth, that pretty pussy and your tight little ass are ours."

The two of them stare at my pussy, watching Leo's fingers. He fists my hair, pulling my face back to look up at him as he pinches my lower lips together around the rope. I suck in a breath, losing myself in his eyes. "You want to come, Pet?" His voice is gentle. Loving. And completely at odds with his hands. He jiggles his grip on my labia, fucking me with that devilish rope.

"Yes, please," I whimper. A wave of pulsing heat floods my core and threatens to wash me away. "Please, sir." I correct myself before he can slap my pussy again.

Leo laughs softly and brings our foreheads together. I'm panting, but Leo's breath is slow and deep; the faintest hint of whiskey warming my cheek. "Soon. Show them that pretty pussy. Show them what they're missing." Two thick fingers slick between my folds before scissoring open. A flood of cool air hits my sex as he uses his grip on my hair to make sure I'm watching his compatriots.

Thorin, unhurried, steps closer, his fingers lazily gliding up and down his hard length. Mal prowls toward me, the ridges of his abs catching the dim light. He licks his lips like he's about to make a meal out of me. Oh, sweet god. I think a single lick might be enough to make me explode. Mal's voice fills the air. "Drip, drip, drip… look at that juicy cunt clench."

Leo scoots out from behind me, but his hand remains on my back, gliding over my shoulder as he circles me. The physical connection between us tugs at something invisible in my chest, but I ignore it, focusing on the giants towering over me. God knows this isn't about emotion. The air in the room goes thin, vibrating with the intensity rolling off of them. Or maybe I'm just trembling.

Mal pulls me forward until I'm lying with my back on the mattress, my head hanging off the foot of the bed. His hand is firm behind my neck, supporting it. I blink up at him, his body looming in front of me, the rest of the room upside-down behind him He flicks at the strap behind my head, and the gag slackens. He tosses it aside before tapping my cheek with his dick. "Don't close that mouth."

I do as I'm told, opening wider. The fleshy crown presses past my lips, slicking along my tongue and painting it with salty pre-cum. I hum. "Oh... good girl," Mal groans, cupping my head in both hands and leaning over me to get a deeper angle. He works farther down my throat, praising me with every thrust. I close my eyes, willing my throat to relax as I swallow around him. Fingers tangle in my hair, tugging hard enough to make my scalp tingle.

Hands slide under my ass, moving the rope, and then there's a mouth on me, a tongue plunging inside my core. Someone flicks at my nipples, over and over until I'm breathless and moaning around Mal's dick.

Fingers replace the tongue, and pressure curls in my belly... just not enough to push me over the edge. I struggle to keep my legs open against the overwhelming pleasure. My pussy throbs, but whoever is between my legs is unrelenting. Feral groans mix with the wet sounds he's making in me. His whole face is buried in my juices, but he's not satisfied.

Something clicks to the rope at my knee. Something cold, and metallic. I try to twist my head to see, but it's impossible. My legs are forced wider and there's a matching click and chill at my other knee. When he lets me go, I realize I can't close my legs. Like not even an inch. A shiver of excitement grips my spine.

I know I said I wanted to try a spreader bar, but this is even hotter than I'd imagined. Someone grabs it, drawing my knees toward my shoulders, and if I thought I felt exposed earlier, it's nothing compared to this. I'm dissolving into a puddle of sensation. Hot breath. A shiver of delight. It's fucking perfect.

Something warm and wet grazes my anus, sending shockwaves of heavenly pleasure through me. A tongue. Oh, sweet god in heaven. It swirls and flicks, the tip pressing inside me with a gentle stretch.

"You gonna let her come or are you going to keep playing with your meal?" The words reach my ears, muffled and distant through the haze of need drowning me, but all I can do is moan plaintively around the dick stretching my throat.

A finger presses against the tight ring of muscle, slippery and warm as it invades. "Nah…" the reply is teasing, almost smug. Thorin. Definitely Thorin. "She hasn't even started begging yet."

MALLON

Jesus Christ, Bree is a sight. I use my grip on the spreader bar to pull her knees almost all the way up to her shoulders. The web of rope that crisscrosses her tan skin pulls taut as her neck stretches to swallow my cock. I grab one of her perfect, bouncy tits, pinching her nipple before giving it a little smack.

She moans enthusiastically, swallowing around me like a silky fist every time I go deeper. I keep having to close my eyes and think of every boring thing under the sun just to keep from spurting down her throat.

"Fuuuck," I mutter, stroking her silky hair. The sleek ponytail is long gone, her dark strands hang loose, brushing my calves. She hums at my touch, like the affection makes her body sing. I jerk my head at Leo and Thorin, getting their attention before petting her again.

"Mmmm." They watch her body intently as her throat vibrates around me. I know what ignorant people think of doms. That we're all looking for someone to smack around under the guise of consent. That we're savage and uncaring. The wolf in sheep's clothing. I'm not saying there aren't doms out there that deserve the scrutiny, but for me — for all three of us — the satisfaction of BDSM is dialing in on a sub's desires. Peeling back the layers of bullshit we all carry around to uncover what she hides deep in her soul. That, and making them come like a fire hydrant being flushed on a summer's day.

Thorin nods, his tongue buried in her ass. Leo's lips twitch in a soft grin. He steps next to me, his monster dick whipping around like a baseball bat.

Show off.

I gesture for him to take her mouth and pull out with a little pop. The second I do, my balls start aching, brutally chastising me for giving her over. She looks up at Leo and I, cheeks flushed as she opens wide, her tongue sticking out eagerly.

Leo stands to her right and holds his dick above her mouth, making her reach for it with that little pink tongue. My feet fuse to the mat, my hand going to my throbbing hard-on at the sight of her. She licks the underside, and swirls her tongue around the head, trying to draw him closer. Her lips stretch around his girth as she takes him deeper.

"Jesus," Leo rumbles, steadying himself on the edge of the cushion like his knees might give out. His eyes roll back in his head. I hear him mutter something about 'dick-taking savant' and chuckle. He's not wrong.

Thorin brings Bree's hips back down to the bed, and rests his palms on the backs of her thighs. She moans around Leo, who utters a string of truly impressive swears.

I push one slippery finger into her, careful not to hit Thorin in the face as I add a second. Curling my fingers, I search out her g-spot, zeroing in on it so fast it's not even funny. We've got her blood pumping good and hot. I stroke my fingers in and out of her at a leisurely pace. No sense in rushing a good thing. She watches me in her periphery with puppy dog eyes. If looks could beg, that one would be on its knees. When I don't speed up or increase the pressure, she whimpers around Leo's dick.

"Good girl," he grunts his praise, fisting her hair in one hand for leverage. The other strokes her cheek, and she leans into it subtly. "So good... God, you suck that dick so good."

"Mm-hm." Bree is panting, body strung tight. Her wrists strain against the rope, fingers reaching at the empty air. I lay my palm over the back of her hand, threading my fingers between hers and give her a gentle squeeze.

Leaning down, I look her right in the eye. "You want to come *so bad*, don't you?"

She moans an ascent, the best she can do with Leo's hog in her mouth. "Tell you what," I offer. "If you can suck Leo dry, maybe we'll let you come. Take all his cum and swallow it down like the greedy little whore you are."

Bree's pussy clenches around my fingers, and from the way Thorin is growling, doubling down his efforts, I'd say he felt that too. Eager to please, or maybe just eager for an orgasm, Bree's head bobs, drawing Leo so deep that his dick disappears completely, and his legs nearly buckle.

"You're such an asshole," Leo grunts and stares at the ceiling, a pained grin on his face, but Bree's eyes shine with a smug sort of pleasure. Brat.

"I think you'll recover," I snark back. Truly, the dude has the fastest fucking refractory period I've ever seen. He'd make seasoned porn stars jealous. Five minutes, and he'll be right back at it.

Thorin presses an oiled-up finger to her asshole, slowly sinking deeper. "Fuck, you've got a tight ass," he grunts, adding a second finger. He twists his fingers, stretching her puckered hole.

She squirms, moaning around Leo's cock. Brat or not, I can't take my eyes off of her. Those dark eyes track each of us, devouring every detail. Her pussy is sopping, rewarding me with little gushes when I hit that spot just right. I have to keep reminding myself to slow down. The temptation to finger fuck her until she soaks the studio is real. Her thighs glisten with it in the dim light. Leaning down, I lap at her honey, cleaning the soft curve of her thigh and the inner crease of her hip with my tongue.

Leo lets out a guttural groan as he goes off, his fingers flexing in the hair he's tangled at the back of her head. Bree watches him, her eyes wide, and again, I get the impression she's trying to memorize every detail. Leo pulls out and, legs shaking, drops to his knees. He leans over her, stroking her hair and whispering praise. She eats it up, leaning into his touch and practically purring like a kitten.

Thorin lifts his chin toward me, giving me a heads up before he lowers her back to the cushion. "I think our pet earned her reward. Mal?" He raises an eyebrow at me. I nod, giving her a long look before rolling her over. With her forearms bound to her calves, and the bar spreading her thighs, Bree can't do much more than whimper as I position her. Her cheek and shoulders press into the cushion, her juicy ass high in the air.

She trembles and lets out a moan as I push my ring and middle finger back into her sweet pussy. My fingers make a squelching sound in her juices, and I feel her tense up. "Ah fuck, that's sexy," I growl, leaning over and giving her curvy peach of an ass a bite. "Such a dirty, wet girl."

Bree moans, relaxing into my touch again. I put more pressure on her g-spot, my whole arm moving with each thrust. Thorin and Leo run their hands over her body, nails scratching, fingers grasping. Leo spreads her ass cheeks, fingering her little pucker.

"How much dick do you think you can take in these tiny little holes, Bree? Should we find out?" I murmur, giving her ass a smack. She clenches around my fingers, her pussy pulsing, fluttering, teetering on the edge.

"We're going to make you come over and over. You know that right? You're going to have to beg us to stop. We're going to take turns fucking this tight little pussy. We're going to fuck you *hard*, fill all these sexy little holes until us cum is dripping out of you—spilling down your pretty legs so everyone knows what a filthy little whore you are for us."

Thorin squats down, putting his nose an inch from hers and wrapping his hand around her throat. He murmurs praise and squeezes, slowly increasing the pressure. Bree stares into his eyes, transfixed, and lets out a plaintive, mewling little moan that makes my dick drip. He stares back, keeping his expression intentionally inscrutable, but whatever passes between them, it's not nothing.

Bree's trembles grow into full body shaking. "Good girl," I growl, spanking her ass hard enough to leave a palm print. "Give it to me." She pants, nodding her head in tiny little jerks at whatever Thorin is saying before turning her face toward me.

Her eyes are pleading as her lips part on a silent scream. Her lashes flutter, her deep eyes rolling back in her head. I'm fucking aching, the blood pounding in my ears. The need to come—to feel her hot, slippery pussy wrapped around my dick—eclipses almost everything else. Almost. I still can't tear my gaze away from her.

Just when I thought she couldn't get any fucking sexier, her pussy floods. My fingers make wet, obscene sounds as her tight little cunt clenches them in a death grip. I smack her ass again and she *screams* her release, writhing against the rope and gushing all over my hand.

Fuck, she's sexy. My balls tighten up and my dick throbs, threatening to spurt all over her, but I get control of the eager bastard. Bree trembles, her body slack on the cushion. I pull my fingers free of her sopping pussy and reach around, putting them between her lips.

12

BRIELLE

I have officially died and gone to heaven. My body thrums with the last vestiges of the orgasm that ripped through my body like a goddamn tornado. A deep voice works its way through my post-orgasmic cloud. "Clean up your mess." Fingers press between my lips, wet and tangy. "Good girl. That's it. Lick them clean."

I do as I'm told, and when he's satisfied, Mal pulls his fingers out of my mouth, dragging along the inside of my lower lip. I open my eyes to see Thorin, still watching me. His fingers stroke my neck, my shoulders and down my arms. He slips a finger under the ropes binding my forearms to my calves, checking the tightness, I think. Someone checks the ties on my other side, but I can't turn my head to see who it is.

"How are your hands and feet?" Thorin asks. "Any numbness or tingling?"

"No, sir," I reply with a languid grin. His lips quirk at one side, the barest hint of amusement. Satisfied, Thorin cups my jaw and gives me a long, slow, soul-deep kiss. After an orgasm like that, I should be satisfied, but when his tongue strokes alongside mine, tasting me with tortured patience, the heat comes roaring back in my belly. It screams for more. For everything.

I want them to fuck me.

I want them to use my body.

I want to be at their mercy while they fill every last inch of space inside of me.

Suddenly, I'm jolted by a loud alarm, my eyes flying open. Thorin breaks away from our kiss, his eyes wide and concerned. Emergency lights flash by the door as the siren wails.

Oh, Jesus. "Is that a fire alarm?" I ask. I can hear the panic rising in my own voice, matching my racing, anxious heartbeat.

"Fuck," Thorin growls. "Do. Not. Move," he tells me sternly, standing and going for his bag.

"Where the fuck would I be able to go?" I call after him. "Unless I roll out of here using my chin to steer, I'm kind of at your mercy!" If I wasn't terrified of burning to death, tied up in a sex club, I'd be lusting after the sight of his tight, bare ass and thick thighs. But as it is, sexy vibes are officially off the table.

"Get her dress!" Thorin barks at Leo, who has already scooped it up along with my shoes and bag. I watch. Because it's all I can do. Thorin retrieves two pairs of medical scissors. He hands one pair to Mal, and they both start snipping the ropes binding my legs and arms.

They work quickly, though nothing can feel fast enough when a fiery death may be imminent. Hands slide under the rope, protecting my skin from getting scratched by the scissors. Someone has the decency to cut the ropes that run between my legs, and thank Christ, because before I know it, they have me sitting up.

Someone pulls my dress over my head, getting it situated before yanking up the zipper at my side. Leo kneels in front of me, still nude, and straps my heels back on my feet. He pulls me up by my hands and steers me toward the door. I look over my shoulder and catch Mal watching me, a deep, concerned frown storming up his handsome face as he throws a shirt on and jumps into his slacks.

"Wait—" I start, not wanting to leave them. Leo throws the door open. People are emerging from the other rooms, just as rumpled, half-dressed, and confused as I feel.

I turn back to Leo, ready to argue, but his expression is gentle, pleading. "We're right behind you. We'll meet you outside, okay?" He presses me through the door. "Go now."

Not that I have a choice. Once he gets me past the doorway, I'm swept away by the other evacuees. *Fine,* I think, grinding my teeth. I'm not going to push against the crowd and get anyone hurt. They better hurry up and put their fucking pants on.

The summer air hits my skin as I step out onto the sidewalk. The whole building is being evacuated. Singles and couples hurry out the front doors, directed by one of the attendants I recognize from the front desk. I try to stay near the front, but I get told off and directed to move down to the end of the block and across the street.

Huffing, I cross the street and wait at the far corner, watching for three, familiar hulking shapes. Firetrucks line the street in front of the club, their sirens deafening. After the dim light inside, the flashing lights are so intense they make my headache. And then there are more sirens, getting louder and brighter by the second.

I watch as the area is flooded with marked and

unmarked Chicago P.D. cruisers, more fire trucks, and several huge black SUVs. They block traffic for two blocks in every direction, a wall of abrasive light and sound. Police officers try to push all the onlookers, myself included, to leave. Apparently, a block from the entrance isn't far enough.

People trickle out of surrounding buildings, but it's mostly cleaning staff, thanks to the late hour. I'm desperately trying to stay where I am, hoping the people moving around me are enough cover, but no such luck. One particularly burly cop points at me when I don't leave right away. "Lady, ya gotta clear the area."

I'm so baffled. There's no smoke. No fire. What the hell is wrong? "My—" I swallow, wondering if the officer knows what that particular building houses. "—friends are inside. I'm not leaving."

His eyebrows, so bushy they look like black caterpillars, lift but his eyes glance down. It's only a microsecond. An involuntary glance. But that little look is all it takes to remind me of the state I'm in. *Oh. My. Fucking. God.*

I stare at the officer, horror flooding my blood stream. My dress is a rumpled mess; wrinkled and not even on my body straight. All those hands in my hair reduced my once-sleek ponytail to a veritable rat's nest, and worst of all, *I'm still wearing the teal rope.*

They cut the ropes binding my arms and legs, and snipped the torturous little knot, but underneath my very tight and very thin black dress, a corset of expensive cord still hugs my body. I have *zero* doubt that the outline is visible through the fabric. Even if it wasn't, it's kind of hard to miss the rope hooked around my neck and tied at my collarbone.

I hug my arms around my body, my skin flushing. I

wish I had a fucking jacket. The officer sighs, and I guess he decides to take pity on me. "Just—just stay here for a minute. Okay?"

I nod and watch as he jogs away, disappearing into the sea of flashing lights. He reappears a couple of minutes later with a gray bundle in his arms. He shakes it out as he gets closer and holds it out for me to take. It's a blanket. An itchy, ugly-as-sin blanket, but a blanket just the same. I take it, thanking him as I wrap it around me, covering the collar of rope.

"Eh, don't thank me. I jacked it from one of the fire trucks," he says, grinning at the stamped letters on one corner. C.F.D. "Look, I need you to get behind the barriers. I'm sure your friends made it out safely. Give it a few and try their cells. Okay?"

I nod, not willing to admit that I don't know any of their last names, let alone phone numbers. I take my pilfered blanket and retreat a couple of blocks, still searching the crowd of onlookers for Mal, Thorin, and Leo. A small team of officers go in the front doors, and I hear whispers from some of the people around me.

Bomb squad.

My first thought is: *What the actual fuck?* My second: *Holy shit, they're in for a surprise.* When I think about what they're going to find inside, I almost want to laugh. The idea of them clearing rooms adorned with whips, paddles, and spanking benches is just too ludicrous. I wait, hoping it will be over quickly, and I can go back inside.

I wait. And wait. And wait. My feet start to ache in my heels, my calves cramping. I'm hungry, tired, thirsty, and sore, but still I wait. I sit down on the curb to give my feet a break, but when I do, a flash of heat races through my body. Fucking Leo with his flogger.

I put my face in my hands, laughter bubbling out of me. This is just… the most ridiculous thing that has ever happened to me. I cross my arms, resting them on my knees as I glance around. The crowd of onlookers is growing. Any chance I had of finding my—no, I correct myself—those men, flew out the window when I left without them. I should have waited. I *knew* it was a bad idea, I just *really* wasn't thinking clearly. Mind-blowing orgasms will do that to a girl, I guess.

Finally, I give up. I'm not going to find them, and they aren't going to find me. I trudge down a side street, getting some distance from all the commotion. I'm only a couple blocks from my office, and considering the state I'm in, that's probably a better idea than hailing a cab.

13

LEO

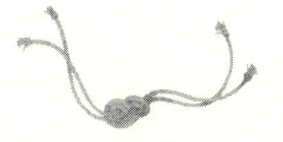

I race down the stairs, my heart pounding as I take them two at a time. Mal and Thorin thunder along behind me. When we get to the ground floor, we're directed out a fire door at the side of the building. The second we step outside, my eyes sweep the crowd for Bree. We can't be more than a minute or two behind her, but she's nowhere in sight. I call her name, but don't get a response.

We're in a small, dark alley between buildings and it's packed with Club Sin members in varying states of dress, all hurrying away from the building. Some go toward the front, most head to the back of the building, splitting off to the right and left.

"Fuck," Mal mutters behind my right shoulder. 'Fuck' is right. In my haste to get her out of the building safely, I sent her outside, on her own, right in the middle of a scene with zero fucking aftercare. And now that we're outside and there's no god damn fire or smoke in sight, I'm pissed. I'm pissed at the club, I'm pissed at the situation, I'm pissed at Thorin and Mal for not being any better than me, but mostly I'm pissed at myself. I — *we* — know better.

"Spread out," Thorin says, his voice thick. "Leo head to the front. Mal, circle to the left, I'll go right. Text if you find her." Thorin takes off, jogging through the crowd. I scrub my palm over my face and turn to head up the alley in the opposite direction, but a hand on my shoulder stops me.

"Stop beating yourself up," Mal says. "We'll find her. She'll be okay."

"You don't know that. She could be fucking dropping right this second. If we don't find her—" The words come out harsher than I meant, but Mal doesn't hold it against me.

"I know. We'll find her."

14

BRIELLE

I hurry to the elevator bank of my building, thankful that the cleaning staff left hours ago. I caught my reflection in enough windows to know I look like a tornado survivor. In the silent building, every footstep echoes and seems to magnify without bodies to absorb the sound.

The elevator dings as it reaches my floor. I peek my head out, making sure the hallway is spectator free, and when I'm sure the coast is clear, I speed walk to the photography studio. The second I'm inside, I drop the itchy blanket and hit the lights. Racks of clothes are lined up in the corner and the sight of them is almost enough to make me weep for joy. We were shooting for fall, so there are cozy lounge pants, bralettes, and sweaters so soft they'd make baby bunnies jealous.

I grab what I need and head for the changing area. Under the bright light, I finally get a good look at myself. My hair is every bit as bad as I thought, and the rope under my dress is even worse. The clingy fabric highlights each knot, every line.

"Oh, lord," the soft moan is about all I can muster, but I gave that cop an eyeful. There is nothing subtle about the rope looped around my neck and disappearing under the neckline of my dress.

Pressing my fingertips to my temples, I take a deep breath. This is insane. How in the hell did my night end up like this? Jesus. I just wanted to try Shibari and maybe get a decent orgasm out of the night. Is that so much to ask? I got my orgasm, sure, but after doing the most extreme walk of shame I can possibly imagine, I have to ask myself — was it worth it?

I sigh heavily. It really fucking was. I would do it again in a heartbeat. Maybe without the walk of shame part, and definitely skipping the scratchy blanket, but the rest of it? Holy hell. One interrupted night of filthy, amazing foreplay, and now I'm hooked.

Stripping my dress off and tossing it on the floor, I examine the remains of Thorin's handiwork. I didn't get a very good look at the club, and it occurs to me that maybe I should have asked… I will next time, I decide. *If* there's a next time. This was supposed to be one night. It's a little presumptuous of me to assume they want to keep playing with a complete newbie. Not when there are so many people at Club Sin with more experience, more knowledge, more… I dunno. Kinkiness?

The sliced tails of cord hang around my thighs, the ends frayed in soft tufts, but the rest of his art is still intact. The way it winds around my body is incredible. I turn, lifting my hair and looking over my shoulder at the column that winds down my back. It's gorgeous. Just the sight of it is enough to send my heart racing all over again. I've never felt this sexy in my entire life.

I'm sorely tempted to wear it all night, but then what?

It's not like I can walk around the office with this under my freaking blouse. No, it has to come off.

I sigh and gather my hair into a messy bun before reaching around to the column at my back. My fingers tug at the knot above the frayed ends, but I can't loosen it. I try to start where Thorin ended, but the ends are concealed in the intricate web somewhere, and after half an hour of fruitless struggling, I have to admit defeat. Not an easy thing for me to do, but my arms are tired, and this office is going to be packed in six hours. At the very least, I need a nap before I face the rest of my day.

I grab a pair of scissors from a workstation and return to the full-length mirror, trying to decide how to get out of the harness while doing the least amount of damage to it. It's too beautiful to just hack at it. Eventually, I have to admit that there's no saving it. Not unless I want to call my assistant to untie me at 2 am. Hard pass on that one. Kelly would swallow her tongue if she knew how I spent my night.

I scrunch my eyes and cut the ropes that run along my side, pulling them free instead of slicing them as much as I can. The loop around my neck is the last to go. With all of the cord piled at my feet, I stare at my reflection, heart pounding like a battle cry. My skin still carries the ghost of the destroyed harness; beautiful, twisted rope impressions mark my body, but I know they'll fade.

Grabbing my phone out of my bag, I pose and snap a couple pictures, something I've never once felt the urge to do before. Maybe I'm just emotional and over-tired, but the thought of letting them vanish fills me with sadness. This way, I can at least keep a memento.

I turn and admire the reminder of Leo's punishment. Red lines slash over my butt cheeks and down my thighs.

Even though they're slightly raised, it doesn't hurt. My skin feels heated and at the slightest touch, my body hums with awareness. I'm surprised at how much I like it.

And he wasn't wrong. Every time I sit, he's going to be all I can think about.

The sun warms my skin, but I'm too cozy to open my eyes. I pull my blanket up and roll over, but instead of finding comfort, the world lurches sideways, and I hit the floor. "Ow…" I mutter. My office door flies open, and Kelly charges in.

"Who's in here — Bree? What — why are you on the floor? Did you sleep here?" She takes a good look at me, her frown deepening. "Jesus, are you okay? You look like hell."

I laugh and get to my feet. "Yeah. I'm fine. I just had a late night downtown, and I couldn't get home."

"Because of the bomb threat?"

My stomach lurches and, for a split second, I think she must know where I was last night… and by extension what I was doing. But then I realize it must be all over the news. No way that would have escaped national news, let alone local.

I nod. "Crazy, right?"

"Insane! I was listening on my way in. They haven't found anything." Figures. The best night of my life got interrupted because some bored jackass wanted to pull a prank. Kelly frowns again. "Bree, did someone hurt you?"

"What? No." I mean, yes, but I totally asked for it. She stomps toward me and grabs my arm. It's only then that I realize Thorin's rope marks didn't *all* fade as fast as I'd expected. Around the outside of my arms, red lines run parallel to each other, all the way from wrist to elbow. They're barely visible up higher, but down near my wrists, where I had a bit more room to struggle, the marks are darker.

I put my arms behind my back, trying to hide the evidence of my night. But it's too late — Kelly got a good look. "Brielle! These are rope burns. How can you stand there and tell me no one hurt you when I can see the evidence for myself?"

"Fine! Yes, it's rope burn, but I asked for it." Deep in my heart, I love that I'm wearing the evidence of last night. But the last thing I need right now is my assistant thinking I'm in some kind of abusive relationship that she needs to protect me from. I'm ninety-nine percent certain she'd go scorched earth. Odds are good someone would lose a testicle.

"You can't blame yourself. If you're a vict—"

"No. Kelly, I literally asked them to tie me up. For fun." I press my fingertips against my eyes. I seriously can't believe I just said those words to my assistant.

"Oh... OH! Oh, my God, I'm so sorry. I didn't mean to overstep... wait... *them?*"

Oh, fuck me and my big mouth. "Long story. Do you have coffee ready? I'm dying."

"It's brewing," she says archly. "But you're just going to completely skate past the part where you said multiple people tied you up last night? At your request?"

"Yep."

"Withholding, much?" she mutters, turning to get my coffee.

"Nosy much?" I call after her with a laugh. She's back in five minutes with a steaming cup of black coffee and a garment bag. She sets the coffee down on my desk and holds out the garment bag.

"Here, I found this in the studio. You need something to cover those arms if you're going to sit through all your meetings today without questions."

"Thank you," I say, taking the bag. "Wait, how many meetings do I have?" I ask with a frown. I don't remember scheduling anything.

"Eleven," she says with a wince. "Thirty minutes with each of the local marketing firms that are available. It was only going to be ten meetings, but a friend got me in touch with a brand-new firm. She says their work is incredible."

"I don't know about new…" I worry my lip with my teeth. "I'd like someone with experience."

"Oh, they have experience, they worked for Gruber and Sons before opening their own firm. If you don't want to see them, I can cut them from the day."

"No, let's keep it. You never know, right? Thank you, Kelly. You're a rockstar."

My day *drags* by. I should be focusing on my meetings. That pesky little thing called marketing is what keeps businesses afloat, after all. But my mind is wandering like a drunk frat boy in an unfamiliar city. Thank God Kelly is taking notes and kicking my foot when I zone out. I should give her a raise.

Per my request to keep our situation quiet, Kelly didn't tell anyone what they were pitching. She just asked them to bring portfolios and told them it's a women-centric apparel company. It's clear some people listened. They come armed with examples that are actually a great fit. Others though... Not so much.

I'm on my sixth cup of coffee by meeting number ten, and as Jackson and associates present a campaign they recently launched for a trendy toothbrush company, my mind drifts. Leo tugs my hair, forcing me to look up into his bottle green eyes. Eyes so deep I could drown in them. Thorin's hands stroke my torso, pulling the ropes snug. His hand squeezing my neck, telling me how pretty I am when I come; what a *good girl* I am for him.

And oh my god. Mal's voice. That gravelly rumble that echoed in my soul. *You're going to have to beg us to stop. We're going to take turns fucking this tight little pussy.* "...As you can see, the subscription model tripled sales of the replacement toothbrush heads, and customer satisfaction actually increased by a factor of..." *We're going to fuck you hard, fill all these sexy little holes until our cum is dripping out of you — spilling down your pretty legs so everyone knows what a filthy little whore you are for us.*"

The toe of Kelly's pump jams against the side of my calf under the conference table, and I have to clear my throat to cover the whimper. There is definitely a bruise developing in that spot. I smile at her and try to pay attention to the toothbrush guys.

Finally, and I do mean, *finally*, they wrap it up. I thank them for their time and have Kelly show them out, sagging back into my chair. "God, I thought they'd never finish," I tell her once she returns, a seventh cup of coffee in her hand.

"That's what she said," Kelly responds with a laugh. I chuckle and slide down in my chair with a dramatic moan. "Come on, just one more, then we can duck out for happy hour." Kelly's tone is bracing, but I can't tell if those words are meant for me or if she is giving herself a pep talk.

"I'm sorry I'm a mess today." I take a sip of the fresh coffee, wondering what the lethal limit of caffeine might be and how many more cups I can have before I get too close.

"Bree, I say this with all the love in the world." Kelly places her hands on my desk and leans over it. "You're a disaster today. Did you even listen to the pitches?"

"Yes!" I exclaim, but add a qualifier. "Most of it." Kelly snorts. "You have to admit, those were dry campaigns. They were fine, I guess, but nothing stood out."

"Well, you've got one more to get through. Maybe they'll surprise you."

"Maybe…" I shrug. "But I doubt it."

15

THORIN

Thorin

I yawn and stretch, looking around the bare waiting area we're being held in. Either this company is brand spanking new, or they need a fucking decorator up in here.

"Does baby need a nap?" Mal chuckles, sticking his finger in my mouth and ruining my yawn.

"Mother fucker, I will end you. Who ruins another man's yawn?"

"Hey, we're all exhausted. Leo and I just have the decency to look professional. And you two are the ones who insisted on taking this meeting, not me."

"Yeah, well that was before we lost her," Leo grumps. He was in a sour mood from the second Bree left our sight last night. And after failing to find her, despite searching the crowd and wandering the streets of Chicago for hours, sour turned to anger and frustration. We've been closer than brothers for years, and I've never seen him like this about anything, let alone a woman.

Then again, saying Bree was 'just a woman,' is serious

bullshit. I saw the way he connected with her. Even I felt it. There was something breathtaking about the way she gave herself over to us.

For years, we've shared women. I know a lot of guys couldn't or wouldn't do that, but for the three of us, it's the only way. There's nothing hotter than making a woman moan around my stepbrother's dick while I eat her pussy. There's nothing hotter than fucking a woman airtight. A dick in every hole with the sole aim of making her come so hard she sees Jesus. Nothing in the world.

At least I thought so. But before last night, in all of my memories, the women were faceless. Exchangeable. It was just pleasure for pleasure's sake. We were all on the same page, and everyone left satisfied. But last night was different. And not just because Mal and I got blue balls.

Until last night, it was only physical. None of us ever went looking for a repeat with anyone. None of us ever woke up all pissy over a session ending early either. We would just shrug and move on.

But after losing Bree last night, there's something inside me that feels raw, like a piece of me was carved out and the wound was left to fester. Mal is surlier than usual, which is really saying something. Even Leo, who is usually all laughs, is being a grumpy motherfucker. I think it's fair to say that none of us are coping well today.

"Gentlemen?" The woman who put us in the holding tank opens the door and gets our attention. She gestures for us to come with her. "Ms. Guerrero will see you now." Leo raises his eyebrows at me in a 'let's get this over with' expression.

Mal takes the lead but I'm noodling that name around. Guerrero. I know I've heard it before. "Isn't Guerrero Spanish for warrior?" I whisper to Leo.

"How should I know? I grew up in Minnesota. You know I'm black and not Spanish, right?"

I roll my eyes. I need a drink. We're led through a lobby, and unlike the holding room, it is actually furnished. Lots of cream-colored chairs and couches, white and tan accents. If I'd ever been to a spa, this is about what I'd expect. Except for the logo that juts out from the reception desk, backlit with bright white light.

JustCloth.

I tap Leo's arm and point at the logo. He's already squinting at it, his head turned like he's trying to place it too. And no wonder. I read an article on the brand's launch a couple years ago, and I'm pretty sure Leo is the one that forwarded it to me back when we were worked for Gruber.

"Sustainable women's fashion supporting female and minority makers," I mutter under my breath. He nods thoughtfully. My wheels are already spinning, cataloging different pitches we could play with, but something else is needling me. Guerrero... what was the CEO's first name? It's on the tip of my tongue, but just out of reach.

I scratch my head, and then, just as the assistant opens the door to a conference room, it clicks. Brielle Guerrero. Daughter of Spanish immigrants, first generation. Started her company in a garage and turned it into a mini empire. Clothes, shoes, makeup, skincare.

One of the photographs from the article comes to mind. Maybe I'm conflating a memory with a wish, but I don't think so. A tall, gorgeous woman with ebony hair and a smile that could cause pileups on the freeway was standing in the middle of an industrial warehouse while activity buzzed around her.

I stop dead in my tracks, heart battering my ribs from

the inside as Leo crashes into my shoulder. "What the hell is—" he whispers, but then the assistant steps out of the way, and Mal and Leo see exactly what I realized two seconds earlier.

Bree. She's standing by one of the chairs, leaning over a laptop. Her crisp white blouse has a collar that buttons up the front of her throat. The throat that I squeezed as I watched her come apart less than 18 hours ago.

Her dark hair falls around her shoulders in natural waves and the makeup from last night is long gone. Our little vixen from last night looks more like a Sunday school teacher, but she's still just as tempting. Maybe more so, because I'd love nothing more than to corrupt every inch of her.

Bree glances up with a forced smile, but the second she sees the three of us in the doorway, her skin goes white as her demure little top. She stares at us, lips parted in shock. Her eyes, so wide you'd think we were here to hurt her, bounce between me, Leo, and Mal. She swallows against her collar, and I feel my lip twitch. The only collar I want on her delicate little neck is ours.

"Lockwood, Lockwood, and Carris." The assistant, seemingly oblivious to the roomful of tension, introduces us. Mal is frozen in place, and Leo is openly gawking, so I step forward, trying to get a handle on the impulse to drag Bree over the table and chain her to my side.

"Nice to meet you," I hold my hand out. "Thorin Lockwood." Brielle eyes my offering like a coiled snake that could spring at her without a moment's notice.

The assistant finally seems to be catching on that something is amiss. She elbows Bree in the side, jolting her out of her reverie. Bree raises her hand toward mine. Slowly. I guess I'm the venomous snake in this situation.

ROOM THIRTY

My fingers clasp around hers, enveloping them. Her warmth gets under my skin, inching through me until I'm burning. I stroke the back of her hand with my thumb, a triumphant current running through me when her pupils flare, and she visibly shivers.

"Brielle Guerrero." Her voice lilts over her last name with hints of a Catalan accent I hadn't noticed before now. My mute compatriots finally find their sacks and step up, introducing themselves, rather unnecessarily. She takes each of their hands in turn, making pleasantries that don't quite meet her eyes. Still, just watching them touch her is enough to make my dick stir.

"Kelly, I could use a cup of coffee. Could you grab a round from Starbucks downstairs?" I glance at the steaming mug sitting on her desk, chock full of coffee. The assistant does too, but she barely misses a beat.

"Uhhh, of course. How do you like your coffee, gentlemen?"

"Black," we answer in unison. She gives us a nod and slips out. The second the door shuts, Bree drops the act.

"What the fuck?" She hisses. "What happened last night? I sat on a fucking corner for like an hour, half-dressed and still in your fucking rope. I had to cut myself out of it and sleep here. Where were you? Did you even try to find me?"

Bree rattles off her questions with an intensity that makes my blood race in my veins. Fuck me, she's sexy. "You're feeling fiery today." She stares at me with a deadpan expression, daring me to utter another word, but I'm not done. "Of course, we tried to find you. We got shoved out a side door, and we split up to search for you."

"Did you know who I was last night?" Bree's voice is

strangled, and she sounds like she's an inch and one wrong word away from a meltdown.

"We didn't know." Mal finally speaks up. "But even if we had, we'd all still be in this situation. We weren't told the name of the company we were walking into. Maybe if you hadn't kept *us* in the dark—"

"Well, it's not like I knew I was meeting with you today! I mean, what are the fucking odds? Am I supposed to walk around Club Sin asking everyone if they work in marketing? Oh, hello. I'd like to engage in some light kink tonight, but first let me make sure we don't have a business meeting tomorrow."

That raises a couple of eyebrows on our side of the table. "You call that light kink?" I ask. Leo socks me in the arm. "Ow." I scowl at my partner in crime, but he doesn't even look at me. He rounds the table wordlessly, stalking toward her with a heavy purpose in his stride.

Brielle pulls her shoulders back, watching him with guarded suspicion as he approaches her. "What are you doing?" She glances at me. "What is he doing?" Before I can answer, Leo wraps her up in his arms.

"Um…" Bree goes rigid in his arms, but a split second later, her steel spine relaxes. Leo whispers something in her ear, and she shakes her head, hugging him back. "No, it's okay." She leans on his chest, facing away from us. He cradles the back of her head in his palm, his fingers weaving in her hair as he glares at me and Mal over the top of her head.

The fuck is wrong with you? he mouths.

16

MALLON

Leo is scowling at me and Thorin, taking it in turns to scold us with his eyeballs. Ugh. I hate when he's right. That was a next-level douchebag thing for me to say. Guilt rises in my throat. This is why I'm shit with relationships. One or two nights with very little conversation and a fuckload of dirty talk? That's my superpower. Actual human communication? Not my strong suit. But for her, I'll try.

Not because it matters to Leo and not because it's the right thing to do. I'll try because, if I'm being honest, I was scared as fuck when we couldn't find her last night. I'll try because I laid awake until well after I should have been at the office this morning, and all I thought about was *her*. And when I finally drifted off, she was still there, torturing my dreams.

I circle the table, coming up behind her. The closer I get, the more I itch to get my hands on her. Leo releases her, and she turns to look up at me with wary eyes. I stroke my knuckles along her jawline and gather her hair in one fist, using it to tip her face up and arch her body against me. If I'm going to apologize, I'm going to do it as a goddamn dom.

She blinks up at me, pupils blown out, and rosy lips parted, but there isn't an ounce of weakness in her eyes. Fuck me, she's incredible. "Brielle," Fuck, I love the way her name rolls off my tongue. "I'm sorry," I murmur. "I shouldn't have talked to you like that. And I'm sorry we didn't find you. We looked for you all night."

"It's okay… I got a little mouthy, I guess." Her lips quirk up at the corners in a tiny smile.

I release her hair and lean down to whisper in her ear. "That's okay. I liked it."

Thorin saunters over to us, and Bree watches him over my shoulder. He runs his hand along his jaw. "You had to cut my rope, huh?" Bree presses her lips together and picks up a large purse. She unzips it and hands it over to him without a word.

Thorin grins down at the contents. "Remind me to tie your hands behind your back next time, huh?"

Bree's eyes brighten and she lifts an eyebrow, challenging him. "*If* there's a next time."

"Oh, bunny," he says with a devious smile. "You're ours until you say 'red'."

"Even after I slashed your precious rope?" she asks archly.

Thorin drops the bag to the ground and circles her wrist in his hand, pulling her toward him. "Especially after that. I'm just going to have to find a way to keep your hands occupied."

"Mmm…" she hums. "Something tells me you have plenty of ideas."

He holds her wrists in his fists, bringing them to his chest and holding her there. Over the top of her head, I see his eyes go soft. Something feels different when the three of us are with her, but I can't nail it down.

"Endless ideas," he confirms.

Bree's back goes stiff. "Shit, Kelly will be back any second."

Thorin doesn't let her go. Not right away. "Tell us what you want to do. We can leave, but we're not going anywhere without you."

She chews on her lip. "No. I wanted to hear your pitch… but I'm going to do what's best for my company. If you can't handle that—"

"Are you saying we can't fuck you into giving us your account?" Thorin smirks. "Because I always like a challenge."

"That is *exactly* what I'm saying."

I run a hand through my hair. We need this, but it's not going to be a problem. "Our firm is brand new, but we've been doing this forever." Thor turns Brielle to face me and Leo, but wraps an arm around her, his palm lying flat on her stomach, fingers splayed in a possessive hold.

"Thorin was the head of the copy department at Gruber. He might look like a douchebag biker, but his memory is borderline eidetic. He's probably the smartest motherfucker you'll ever meet. Leo was the wizard in charge of the art department. All graphics and video went through him before clients ever saw a thing."

Bree's eyebrows rise, her expression thoughtful. "And what about you? I'm guessing Gruber didn't keep you on just to look at your pretty face."

Thorin leans down, propping his head on her shoulder and grinning at me. "Baby stepbrother over there was their top brand strategist. There's a reason Gruber went downhill the second we left." I grind my teeth. Baby stepbrother my ass. I'm only six months younger than him *and* I'm taller.

Brielle's gaze turns assessing, and I can see her weighing her options. When she speaks, the flirty tone is gone. "Go sit on your side. We'll wait for Kelly and then you'll make your pitch." She's all business and steel, and it is a fucking turn-on.

"I kinda like it when you're bossy," Thor murmurs in her ear before biting her earlobe. Her eyes flutter. "Either way, come home with us tonight."

"I need clothes," she argues. "And a shower."

"We have a shower. A great big one," Leo runs his fingers over his lips, a hungry look in his eyes. "And clothes are overrated."

"You realize you're saying that to the owner of a fashion brand, right?"

"Yeah, but that's not really what you're selling," Thorin argues. Bree frowns at him.

"I think I know what I'm selling," she says archly. Thorin pulls her earlobe between his teeth. He's a bolder motherfucker than I would be right now.

His fingers stroke the collar of her shirt and wrap around her throat. He whispers something in her ear and right in front of my eyes, she melts for him and it's the most beautiful thing I've ever seen.

Thorin releases her, letting her wobble on her feet, drunk on lust. "But like you said, we'll wait for Kelly."

17

BRIELLE

Thorin's fingers tighten around the sides of my neck. His lips graze the shell of my ear as he whispers, "Come home with us so we can finish what we started. I didn't even get a taste of you yet."

I swear, my soul leaves my body for a second. The spice of his cologne invades my senses, and it's all I can do not to whimper as memories of last night stream through my mind. His whispered praise, the intensity of his eyes as he watched me come, telling me what a *good girl* I was for him.

"But like you said, we'll wait for Kelly." His tone is amiable as he releases me, and the sudden shift leaves me weak-kneed. Holy hell.

Shaky, I watch the three of them go back around the table. Thorin with his Viking undercut and tattoos peeking out from under his shirt sleeves and unbuttoned collar. Mallon tugs the cuffs of his suit jacket as he sits, adjusting the cufflinks at his wrists and straightening his tie.

And then there's Leo. Gorgeous Leo with his bottle

green eyes. I might have an extra soft spot for Leo after the way he broke the tension. *I'm so sorry. I never should have let you out of my sight.* The tortured way he whispered those words in my ear is something I'll never forget. He held me like something precious; something he couldn't bear to let go of.

But even in the midst of all that, he was more worried about my comfort than anything else. *Tell me to fuck off if you don't want a hug.* But the second he wrapped his arms around me, I already knew I didn't want him to let go. That was all it took to erase the slow current of unease I've been wading through since the alarm went off last night, and we got separated.

"I have a question." I tap my pen on my notebook and they all look at me expectantly. "How does this work for you three? Like… how do you not kill each other if you work together all day and then go tear it up at Club Sin? You share everything. That just seems kind of… intense."

Thorin grins at me. "You know what they say—"

I hold up a hand and interrupt. "If I hear the words 'work hard, play hard' come out of any of your mouths, I'll call security to have you removed from the building."

"I was going to say, 'sharing is caring.'" Thorin chuckles as I groan and reach for the phone. Mal's too fast though. He drags it out of my reach with a wink.

"Fine, I guess you can stay. Are the three of you… together?"

The three of them kind of shake their heads, but it's ambiguous at best. Leo finally speaks up. "Yes and no. If you're asking if we cross swords, that's a hard pass. But it's still a spectrum. We all share… quirks."

"Quirks?" I repeat. "Like what?"

"We aren't turned off by each other, we just vastly

prefer... you." I can't help smiling at that. That was a delicate way to word it considering I met them in a sex club and from the sound of it, they would have found *someone* if I hadn't been there. Strangely, that doesn't bother me the way I thought it would. I don't mind being the beneficiary of their practice.

Thorin picks up the thread. "Specifically, it's hot as fuck to tie you up and watch you get railed. I don't need to play with his dick," he hooks a thumb at Mal. "To appreciate the look on your face when he makes you come all over it as many times as you can."

"You're such a poet," Leo mutters, shaking his head. My face is on fire. I'm pretty sure I can hear my mascara sizzling.

Just then, Kelly opens the conference room door, and I realize that in my fascination with their answers, I've crawled halfway on top of the table. I clear my throat and lean back in my chair. Kelly is juggling a drink carrier with four coffee cups and a blended something tucked under her other arm.

Mal hops up and takes the carrier off of her hands. "Thank you so much, Kelly."

She beams at me and raises her frozen drink in a funny sort of toast. "And thank you for my sugar fix." Mal holds one of the coffees out for me to take, letting the other two get their own. "Thank you."

Lockwood, Lockwood, and Carris sip their coffees. That's how I have to refer of them here, I think. Otherwise, I'll say Mal's name and be thinking about him fingerfucking me into oblivion.

I pull my chair in and sit down. I wince as my butt hits the chair, cheeks burning as I remember Leo's 'punishment'. I've been so careful all day. I haven't winced once, even though he definitely gave me a keepsake. One that makes me blush every time I think about it. *You're going to remember what happens to naughty pets.* Oh, yes I do. It's just not much of a deterrent.

I glance up to see if they noticed. Oh, boy. They definitely noticed. Thorin presses his lips together and looks down at his tablet. Mallon has the grace to take a sip of coffee, even though the corners of his eyes give him away. But Leo? He lifts his eyebrows, outright smirking at me.

"Are you okay?" he asks me innocently.

"Fine," I reply, looking down at my notes.

"You sure? You kind of winced there. Can I grab you some Tylenol or something?" There's absolutely no mistaking the humor in his eyes as he watches me.

"You're so sweet! Thank you for offering, but it's nothing. Nothing at all. Just a teeny tiny bruise. I really can't even remember how I got it, but I must have done *something*, right?" It's my turn to smirk as his eyes darken with promise.

"I'm sure it'll come to you." He says it casually, but the heat in his gaze is nothing short of volcanic. Oooooh, I'm going to pay for that later. The thought makes my core tighten in anticipation.

I address Thorin and clear my throat, trying to get my mind out of the gutter and back on business. "While Kelly was out, you said I'm not selling clothes. What did you mean?"

"Exactly that. You're selling an idea. A lifestyle. By giving people the chance to shop ethically and educating them on where their garments come from, they feel engaged. Connected with the wider world. Clothes are just the byproduct. A facilitator of that. What really matters is how people feel when they shop with you. Pair that idea with the quality you already have, add in effective marketing, and updated branding… you're looking at a true empire."

Kelly raises her eyebrows at me, sitting straighter than I've seen her all day. This is easily the best pitch I've heard, but I'm glad to see she's on the same page, and it's not just because I'm biased.

"So how would we implement that?" I lean back in my chair and chew on the end of my pen. Three sets of eyes follow it to my mouth. Mallon shifts in his seat, readjusting himself, Leo licks his lips, and Thorin? He shamelessly eye fucks the hell out of me.

Mallon speaks up this time. "We focus on the makers. They're what make your clothes special. Handmade, quality pieces with a story. We run ads on social media, video streaming services, and podcasts with snapshots into different makers. How they perfected their craft. What the sales mean to them, their family, even their community."

Kelly is taking notes, nodding along, and I can't help but agree. "Still ads are trickier. You have to focus on the clothes, but the settings need to be on brand. We need to do more research, but I can guarantee your clients are likely to be earthier and more eco-conscious."

"Yeah," I agree. "That's accurate. If we hire you, you'll have access to the market research we have." I try not to react, but Kelly kicked me under the table the second I said the word 'if.'

I kick her back. I'm awake this time and that bruise is going to be massive already. She snorts out a small laugh but covers it as a sneeze. "Bless you," three deep voices say in unison. She looks up at them, eyes as round as saucers.

I can't blame her. I know from personal experience that the combined force of their personalities, their distinctly alpha energy hits like a sledgehammer. And even though I know she's hung up on someone else, I still frown.

I have to remind myself that I don't get to be possessive or jealous. Whatever the situation between the four of us is, it's just physical. It's temporary and it's just physical. They can look at anyone they want. They can talk to anyone they want. They aren't mine.

I sip my coffee, looking up over the rim. Leo's watching me. No, he's smoldering at me. His foot nudges mine under the table and he winks at me. I don't know how he conveys so much without speaking a word, but his message is clear. *Don't be jealous.*

18

LEO

The clock is ticking closer and closer toward six. As much as I love talking advertising, Brielle's blouse buttons keep catching the light and the impulse to rip her shirt open and send those buttons flying is enough to make me antsy. Sitting across the conference table from her is just too far.

The assistant subtly shows Brielle the time, and our girl runs her hand through her hair. "Oh! Kelly, you've got kickboxing tonight. Right?"

"I do, but I can always go another day." Even I can tell that's not what she wants, and I couldn't be happier to agree.

"I think we're about done here." Brielle makes little shooing motions with her hands. "Go. Have fun. We'll work on contracts Monday morning. Have a good weekend."

Kelly leans over and gives Brielle a hug. "You're sure?" She's already standing and gathering her things as she asks.

"One hundred percent. Say hi to Brian for me."

My relief at seeing the assistant getting ready to leave

evaporates. Brian? Who the fuck is Brian? I'm scowling like a petty little bitch, but I can't help it. And when I glance over at Mal and Thorin, they're wearing identical frowns.

The second Kelly is out the door, Thorin leans over the table. "Who's Brian?"

Brielle, pleased to have the upper hand for a second, arches an eyebrow at him. "That's really none of your business." From the lobby, we hear the elevator ding. Thorin grunts and stands up. "What are you doing?" Brielle asks as he circles the table.

"What's your safe word?" he growls.

Brielle spins in her chair to face him. "Why?" she asks, a grin spreading across her face.

Thor leans over her, his palms pinning her forearms to the chair's armrests. "Because I'm about to put you on your knees and fuck the sass out of that gorgeous mouth while those two watch. And when I'm done, they're going to take a turn."

Brielle glances sideways at Mal and I through lust-hooded eyes and wets her lips. "Is that what you want? You just want to sit there and watch?"

I nod. "For now…" Brielle's eyes flare and her breathing picks up. She squirms in her seat, just a bit, but more than enough to give away her excitement. I'd bet good money on the state of her panties right now.

She looks back up at Thorin. "We need ground rules first."

"New ones or changing ones?" I can practically hear him purring. Dude likes his boundaries. Mostly so he knows how far he can take things. It's like a challenge for him.

"New ones," she breathes. "This is my place of business. Monday through Friday, and sometimes on Saturdays, I'm off-limits from eight am to six pm. You will not interfere with my company or my ability to run it."

The three of us glance at the clock ticking away on the wall. *Tick-tick-tick.* 5:58 pm. "Agreed," Thorin replies. "And by extension of that stipulation, we get you after six."

"For how long?" There's a sliver of vulnerability in her voice. Mal catches it, and I can already tell Thorin's made a mental note of it from the way his expression softens. Some subs tolerate and even enjoy being punished with abandonment, but it's pretty clear that won't sit well with her.

"Day to day? We'll make sure you're well rested, fed, and at work on time every morning except Sunday and the Saturdays you take off. As for long term, I already told you. You're ours until you want out. You can safe word anytime and we'll stop. We'll figure it out. One way or another."

Tick-tick-tick. Shit. That was a leap we should have talked about before he said it. I get that he's not willing to let her go, and I'm right there with him, but Mal, the king of commitment phobia, is going to freak out.

It's not his fault, really. Getting your balls and heart stomped on by a cold-hearted she-devil can do that to a guy. Even one as tough as Mal. *Tick-tick-tick.*

I glance over at him, dreading his reaction and already trying to think of a way to smooth things over. But he doesn't balk at all. Instead, he's watching her face with deep focus and fascination.

Tick-tick-tick. I shouldn't be excited by his reaction, but for the first time in my life, I can see myself with someone. Even better, I could see Brielle with all three of us. I know that's a big fucking leap, but deep in my bones, this feels… different. *Tick-tick-tick.*

Brielle glances at the clock and we all follow her eyes. 5:59 and 50 seconds. *Tick-tick-tick.* She bites her lip and inhales, holding it for so long my heart can't take it.

"Agreed."

19

BRIELLE

Tick-tick-tick. Thorin watches the second hand cross the 12. Then his eyes slide back to mine, the gray of his irises seeming to darken by the breath. "Give me your bag, Pet."

Oh. My. God. The tone of his voice shifts. Gone is the agreeable man I was just setting expectations with. In his place is a Viking in a dress shirt, dead set on making me *his*. I reach down under the table to the purse full of rope. I've carried it with me all day, zipped up and clipped shut, out of fear that someone would find it if I left it alone for more than 3.2 seconds.

Leo rolls backward in his chair, clicking the lock on the door. "You're going to have to keep her quiet," he says lazily.

"Oh, I think I can manage that…" Thorin cocks his head to the side, openly admiring my body. "You know what I thought when I saw you in this sweet shirt, Pet?" I shake my head, unable to look away once he sets his sights on my face. "I thought you looked like a Sunday school teacher. So innocent with these little pearl buttons…"

He leans over me, kissing my forehead, his fingers tracing the line of pearls from my neck, all the way down to the waist of my pants. He rubs the lowest button, slowly swirling it in a tight circle with his index finger. My breath hitches, heat flooding my core as I realize what he's doing.

"I wanted to rip it to shreds. Send those sweet little buttons flying so I could corrupt every last inch of you."

My hips lift involuntarily. Everything is involuntary right now. His eyes have me under a spell, and I let myself go. There's a freedom in it that I've been craving since the second I left them last night.

They can put me where they want. Take me however they want to. Because deep down, I know they'll take care of me. And right now, I love that I don't have to guess what he wants, because I know he'll tell me. He'll demand it. Take it. And he'll make my body sing.

"Such pretty little buttons," Thorin muses, pressing my hips back down into the chair. Slipping his fingers into the waistband of my pants, he flicks it open and slides the zipper down. He finds the next pearl button, rubbing it against my pubic bone in slow, soft circles.

Just below his finger, my clit is throbbing, screaming to be next. "But now you have to wait." He covers my mouth with his hand and flicks his middle finger against my clit with deadly accuracy.

I cry out in shock, but it turns into a moan, muffled by his hand. Movement out of the corner of my eye distracts me. Mallon and Leo are on their feet, unbuckling belts and unzipping pants.

"Pants off, little bunny, but keep the panties." I try not to whine at his words as I lift my hips and push my wide-leg trousers down. Thorin doesn't help. He just crosses his arms and watches me until I've set them aside. "Good girl. Now get on your knees. Hands behind your back." I follow orders, sliding out of my chair and sinking to the carpet, never taking my eyes off him. "Someone is feeling obedient," he rumbles, stroking my cheek affectionately.

He reaches into the bag of rope, pulling out pieces of the teal cord until he finds one he likes. He makes quick work of freeing the leftover knots and kneels behind me, pulling my forearms over each other so my fingers reach the opposite elbow.

There's a gentle stretch in my shoulders and chest as he binds my arms in place. By the time he's done, I can't budge them a single centimeter, let alone an inch. He wraps rope around my ankles, gathers my hair into a ponytail, and lifts my chin with one finger.

I can't really tell what he's doing until he comes back around, arms crossed in satisfaction. He's tied my hair to my arms, and my arms to my ankles, the position forcing my body into an exaggerated arc.

The front of my shirt strains, buttons threatening to pop off on their own volition as I try not to topple over backwards. Thorin puts his foot between my knees and utters one word. "Spread."

I can't move my feet, but I walk my knees outward, finding the act of balancing so much easier. Mal and Leo step closer, and with a whimper I realize they have their dicks in their hands, and they're stroking the rock-hard lengths as they watch me struggle.

Thorin pushes his foot right under my pussy and I gasp as the laces bump along my clit through my underwear. "Don't come." There's no missing the force behind his demand. The subtext. *Or else.*

Thorin undoes his belt, pulling it out of its loops. He

uses his thumb to open my mouth and sets the belt across my tongue. "Be a good girl and hold this for me." The scent of leather fills my nostrils, and I'm fighting the urge to grind against his foot. There's something so… filthy about being used like this, but I don't care. Not when it feels this good.

He shoves his pants down, just far enough to free his cock. It juts toward me, bobbing just out of reach, not that I can get a great look at it. My bindings keep my eyes turned up toward Thorin. He watches me with a dark, heated expression, rolling up his shirt sleeves.

He takes his time, but every now and then he wiggles his foot to send jolts of pleasure coursing through me, smirking when I squirm. When he's finally satisfied that his sleeves won't interfere, he sets his stormy gaze on my shirt. He doesn't rip it off, sending the buttons flying. And as hot as I thought that would have been, what he does is even better.

Thorin reaches down, yanking the fabric roughly as he releases each button. He's so strong that he nearly lifts me off of my knees, and every tug pulls my forward against his foot. I press my lips together and close my eyes, but there's no concealing the way my breath shudders on every exhale.

"Look at me," he demands, stroking my upturned chin with one finger. I open my eyes and find him admiring me. He leans down, tracing the edges of my bra. "I *love* this… more white. How… virginal. Look at you trying to play the innocent. You don't quite pull it off when your nipples beg for attention like that though."

He scrapes his nails over the fabric, teasing me before pinching both of my nipples hard enough to make me gasp around his leather belt. "So pretty," he murmurs.

Something inside of me purrs at the praise. Needing it. Craving it. He takes the belt from my mouth, wiping the edge of my lip with his thumb before looping the leather behind my neck. He holds both ends in front of me, clutched in one hand and strokes my hair with the other.

"Can't have my good girl falling." The sensation of the leather around my neck is incredible; smooth and supple, but firm enough that he could really yank me around if he wanted to. Thorin presses his thumb to my lips, opening my mouth and dragging my bottom lip down with the pad of his thumb.

20

THORIN

Brielle's focus is almost singularly mine. With the exception of little glances toward Leo and Mal, she obediently keeps her eyes on mine. Her pink tongue glistens behind her open lips, and just the thought of sliding my dick against it makes my tip drip. A little splash of precum lands on her breasts and trails down into her cleavage.

"Fuck," I hear Mallon mutter. "We should have done this at the house."

"We can relocate," I reply without looking away from Brielle. "Later."

Using my grip on the belt to hold her steady, I feed my cock between her lips. Wet heat envelopes my head as she sucks greedily, bobbing to pull me deeper. "Good girl," I grate between clenched teeth, working myself deeper. "Take it all, bunny. Swallow me down that tight little throat."

Her eyes shine, but she doesn't pull away. I feel her swallow around me and for a second, I'm afraid I'm going to lose control. Leo and Mal move, standing on either side of Brielle. She blinks up at them through her lashes, eyes widening as she watches them. Neither of them seems to be shooting for the finish line. They just slow stroke it for her benefit.

I pull out, leaving her gasping for air, and lean over her. "Is it my business yet?" Brielle stares up at me, her lips puffy. When she doesn't answer me right away, I put my dick back in her mouth and pull her farther onto it using the belt. She moans. She fucking *moans*.

"If I didn't know any better, I'd say you were enjoying this."

Brielle doesn't look away as she nods. Between my cock in her mouth, and her hair tied to her wrists, calling it a nod might be generous, but there's no mistake. She loves it.

I pull free again, tightening my grip on the belt as I lean over her. "Is it our business now?"

"I don't — I don't remember," she pants. Her eyes are heavy with lust, her cheeks pink. Leo reaches down, pinching her hard little nipple through the see-through white lace. Her breath hitches with a moan, and she grinds shamelessly against my foot.

"You forgot?" I chuckle, releasing the belt from around her neck and stepping back. I swing the tail between her splayed knees, giving her pussy a little tap. She gasps and bites her lip, watching my movements.

For me, the belt is all about the threat; that little trickle of fear that runs down her back. Just knowing how easy it would be to hurt her with it is enough to get her adrenaline pumping. I swing it lazily. *Tap. Tap. Tap.*

By the fifth swing, she's moaning. I lean down and pull her panties aside, swiping a finger along her slit. My finger comes away shining; coated in her juicy pussy. She trembles, watching as I rub her arousal over the head of my dick and shove it back in her mouth.

"How's that cock taste now?" I growl. She bobs harder, moaning around my length. I swear to Christ I almost shoot straight down her throat. I'm not going to make it long. Between the ultimate blue balls last night, and the sounds she keeps making around my dick, I'm riding the edge of a hair trigger.

Grabbing a fist full of her hair, I pop her off my dick one last time, and boop her on the nose with each word I speak. "Who. Is. Brian?"

Brielle's eyes light up with realization and she grins.

"One of the kickboxing instructors at my gym. Kelly wants him baaa—." She draws out the last word, presumably 'bad', but I don't let her finish it before filling her mouth again.

She gives a throaty chuckle, eyes full of mischief now that she remembers why she's being punished. "You are such a brat," I growl, holding her face and thrusting between her lips. She flicks at my piercings with her tongue, and my balls tighten up, a pulsing rush building at the base of my spine.

Brielle's eyes roll back in her head like she can't think of anything she wants more. "Good girl," I groan. "That mouth isn't sassy anymore, is it? Can't talk back with a dick down your throat." She shakes her head, just a fraction of an inch.

"That's it… take it all." My vision closes in, and I grunt. "Good girl. Take that dick and swallow every drop I give you." She lets out a hum, and I can't hold back another second. I push my dick deep down her throat and hold it there, spurting down her throat, my eyes rolling back in my head.

Brielle swallows me down, her throat milking the cum from my cock. My head falls back, and I bite my lip hard enough to taste blood, trying to contain my groan. She sucks and sucks until I'm shaking, my body wrung out.

I pull away and stroke her cheek. When I look down at Brielle, her adorable little lips are pulled up in a smirk. Oh, she is proud of herself. And she should be. "Holy fuck," I whisper, sinking down to my knees in front of her. I reach around pulling the little quick release knot tied in her hair.

Cupping her jaw, I lower her chin slowly. Mascara trails down her cheeks and her eyes are sleepy, but that blissed out smile on her face is all subspace. My heart beats double-time as she blinks at me, and instead of the post-nut clarity I usually feel, I just want more.

21

BRIELLE

Thorin cups my face, easing my neck back to a normal angle. He massages the back of my neck and the base of my skull with the tips of his fingers. "Anything hurting?" he murmurs, gray eyes searching my face.

I shake my head, my body floating. Thorin watches me, and I realize I must be a mess. My eyes are watery, and I can feel the mascara and tear streaks drying under my eyes. But he's not looking at me like I'm a mess. His eyes are tight at the edges, and his hands smooth over my skin like he can't get enough.

"Good." His voice is slow and smooth, wrapping around me like a warm blanket. Thorin presses his lips to mine, giving me a long, drawn-out kiss. My heart stutters, then races to catch up before tripping all over itself. My head swims as he takes his time exploring my mouth.

He reaches around me with both hands, untying my ankles and wrists. The rope falls away, and Thorin pulls me into his lap. He massages my wrists and inspects my hands before moving onto my ankles and feet. He even pulls my blouse back together, fastening a couple of the buttons.

ROOM THIRTY

He dotes on me. There's no other way to put it. His hands move over my skin, every motion filled with gentle affection. This, from the man who just face fucked me for smarting off to him.

The thought makes me snort. Thorin holds my chin between his thumb and forefinger, turning my face up to his. "What's so funny?" he asks, one brow raised.

"You're so..." I trail off, not sure how to put it into words. "Cuddly." He raises both eyebrows at that.

"I can safely say, no one has ever called him that before," Mal chuckles from behind me. I look at him over my shoulder and realize he and Leo have both zipped back up.

"You two done with me already?" I ask, eyeing them with a pout.

Leo laughs out loud. "Oh, not by a long shot. But for what we have in mind... let's just say the conference table isn't ideal."

That sends a shiver up my spine, and when Thorin nips at my neck, the shiver grows into a full-body tremble. "So where are we going?" I whisper, canting my head to the side to give him as much of my skin as he wants.

Thorin licks the length of my neck and bites my earlobe. "You'll see."

Leo drives and Thorin sits up front, but Mal climbs into the back of the SUV with me, and I'm a little surprised. Of the three of them, Mallon is the one that seems... a little less interested in me. Or maybe he's just more closed off. I don't know.

I sure as hell enjoyed his apology though. A little hair

pulling goes a long way in my book. I sit by the window and buckle my seatbelt. A split second later it releases. Confused, I look down, and find Mallon's finger on the button. He lifts that finger and crooks it, beckoning me closer with a hint of a smirk.

Licking my lips and trying to hold back a goofy smile, I slide into the middle seat. Mallon reaches around me and buckles me in before pulling me against his side and wrapping an arm around my shoulders. I lean into him, resting my head on his chest, my heart rapid firing in my chest.

The city zips by. I watch the buildings turn to suburbs, but the only thing I'm focused on is the way Mallon's fingers stroke my arm and play with my hair. He runs them over my neck, traces my collar bone, and brushes his knuckles along my jaw.

There's nothing overtly sexual about his touches, but the message isn't being received on my end. His questing fingers raise goosebumps on my arms and send little shivers down my spine. I'm intimately familiar of what those fingers are capable of, and innocent or not, those gentle touches are excellent reminders of what I have to look forward to.

Fucking Thorin and his teasing. The inseam of my pants rides against my soaked panties ensuring that I feel every tiny bump in the road and don't have a chance to quiet the ache he started. I bite my lip, trying to ignore it, but then my mind wanders to Thorin and his precision with the tail end of that belt…

"You're awfully wiggly, pet." Mallon's murmurs, the baritone of his voice seeping through me.

"Yeah, well…" I try to brush it off with a laugh, but

I'm pretty sure I just sound tortured. Leo glances at me in the rearview mirror with a knowing expression.

Thorin full-on turns around, smirking at me as he makes a tutting sound through his teeth. I press my lips together and tug at the legs of my pants. No point in being stealthy if they can tell that I'm a mess over here anyway.

Mallon chuckles and it's a devious sound. Borderline evil. "Do you need something, Brielle?"

God, I love the way he says my name. "Nope." That didn't sound any less tortured, despite my best effort. Mallon doesn't say anything, but his fingers start toe-curling roving all over again. Thorin flips the visor down, but it's not because the sun is in his eyes. He lifts the cover over the mirror, angling it so he can watch me suffer. His eyes bore into mine, making it impossible to look away.

The pads of Mal's fingers dip under the unbuttoned collar of my shirt, teasing along my collarbone before exploring lower. I glance up at him, but he's watching out the window, completely nonchalant as those fingers stroke my sternum. They caress the swell of my breasts, fingers sliding a fraction of an inch under the lace of my bra.

My heart races, wanting more, but there's the aching frustration of being trapped in the SUV. Thorin watches Mallon's hand move under my shirt and licks his lips. My irritation gets the better of me. I huff, squirming in my seat again, but pressing my thighs together does precisely zero good. Not when Mal's fingers skate lower and Thorin is eyeing me like something to be devoured.

"You're so mean!" I laugh, trying to sit up straight. Mallon isn't having any of it, though. He grips my chin between his thumb and forefinger, tipping my face up in a firm hold.

"I asked if you needed anything, but you said no." His expression is stern, but a little twitch at the corner of his lip belies his hard eyes. "You're going to learn real quick that it's best to be honest with me. Because what I want," he stresses the word and tightens his hold on my chin, making sure I'm paying attention. I'm definitely listening. It's the breathing part that's difficult.

"… is to take care of you. If you tell me you're hungry, I'll feed you. If you tell me you're thirsty, I'll get you champagne. And if you tell me your pussy is soaking wet and your little clit needs some attention, that's what you'll get."

My jaw drops. That is the single sexiest thing I have ever heard. "But if you lie to me or ignore your own needs, you're going to be punished. You know what Thorin up there will do to you?"

I shake my head, well aware that I'm staring at him like a starstruck teenager. Mallon lowers his face to mine. I'm expecting a kiss, but he presses his thumb between my lips, holding my lower jaw like a misbehaving pet. When he speaks, it's just a low whisper, but there's no mistaking who's in charge.

"Thor will tie you up, suspend you from our ceiling, and let you think about your choices. Maybe we'll fuck you, maybe we won't, but you'll have plenty of time to reflect. You've already gotten a taste of Leo's brand, but if you think you're sore after a little flogger play, wait until he puts you over his knee and gets out his paddle. You'll be standing for a week."

Fuck me. I have to keep reminding myself this is punishment he's describing. I get that most women would balk at the idea of being suspended like that; put on display like an interesting light fixture. But just the thought of it adds fresh arousal to the desperate situation between my thighs.

"And me? Oh, pet. I will spool you up, and torture you with orgasms." I try not to grin around his thumb, but the effort makes the muscles in my cheeks twitch; something that Mallon absolutely does not miss. "I can see what you're thinking," he says with a smirk. "You're thinking that doesn't sound half bad, but do you have any idea how long an hour of edging feels?"

I shake my head as much as I can. I really have no clue, and it sounds like death by orgasm... but what a way to go. "

"You'll beg. You'll probably cry. Either way, I'll ignore every plea, every whimper, and every moan until I'm satisfied that you've learned your lesson. And when I finally, and I do mean finally, let you come, it won't just be one and done. No, baby girl. You'll come over and over. One after the other. No breaks. You'll come until I've wrung every last drop of defiance out of you. And then I'll give you one more, just to solidify it."

My panties aren't wet anymore. Nope. I'm pretty sure the Midwest just got a new Great Lake. Mallon releases my jaw, dragging his thumb down my lip. "That's your one and only warning." He claims my mouth, kissing me with a ferocity I've never experienced. My thoughts swirl, a mess of emotions and sensations that I can't untangle. Mallon eases back and stares into my eyes, his nose just an inch from mine. "Do you need something from me, Brielle?"

I lick my lips, already missing the feel of him. I don't have a lot of experience asking for what I want. Not like this. "I—" I bite my lip as my voice wavers. Nope. Nuh-uh. I'm not a wilting flower. I am Brielle motherfucking

Guerrero. "My pussy is soaking wet, and my… clit needs your attention. Sir."

I probably could have left out the sass on 'sir.' I'm sure I'll pay for it later, but I'm finding it hard to care at the moment. A smile spreads across Mallon's face and he raises an eyebrow before glancing out the window. The houses are thinning out, getting larger, and we're well off the highway.

Mallon releases his seatbelt, releases mine, and pulls me into his lap. Before I can even say 'thank you, sir,' he yanks my pants down my legs. I lift my hips and he uses a foot to shove them down to my ankles.

"Put your hands behind my neck," he growls buckling his seatbelt around the both of us. "If they move, you wait until we get home."

I reach back with both arms and lace my finger behind his neck, loving the way the bristly hairs at the base of his skull tickle my palms. Mallon's massive arms cage me against him, enveloping me. I lean back against him, resting my head in the crook of his neck.

He spreads my thighs wide. One hand slips under my shirt, kneading my breasts and the sensitive peaks. His other pulls the sodden panel of my panties to the side. "You weren't kidding," he rumbles, pressing a finger to my entrance and slicking it through my arousal.

My eyelids snap shut, and I suck in a gasp of air as Mallon twists his wrist, plunging that finger inside me with a growl of approval. His lips tug at my earlobe as he buries a second finger in my core. "Fuck, you feel so good." His fingers crook and I let out a shameless moan.

"I can't wait to get my cock inside you," He murmurs, fingers speeding up. "Sink into this sweet pussy…" he presses hard, setting off the barest blip of an orgasm.

"Mal!" I cry out, feeling a gush of moisture coat his fingers.

"Oh, that's my good girl." His arm tightens around me, his fingers pinching my nipple. Pressure builds in my core, but Mal doesn't ease up. "You wanna come for me again, don't you baby?"

"Yes sir," I whimper. Thorin's eyes are fixed on me, a scorching audience of one. I don't know why that pushes the whole scene over into a new category of dirty, but it does. "You remember the rule?" Mal asks me.

I nod and tighten the weave of my fingers. "Good girl. You better hang on." That's the only warning I get before his rhythmic pumping turns frenetic. A brutal wave of pleasure slams into me and I open my mouth in a silent scream, fighting to keep my hands in place.

22

MALLON

B rielle writhes in my arms, her slick juices running down the backs of knuckles as I work my ring and middle fingers up against her g-spot. "You want to come for me, don't you pet?" I ask, knowing full well she's desperate.

"Yes-yes-yes-yes-yes. Sir." I want to chuckle at the way she keeps adding the honorific to the end of her pleas, but I can feel her pussy rippling around my fingers, contracting and reaching for release. I grind my palm down on her swollen clit, a surge of animalistic pride gripping my spine. Brielle keens, her ass grinding in my lap as she falls apart, shaking and trembling in my arms.

I suck her tangy arousal from my fingers and guide her arms down, maneuvering her sideways in my lap. She blinks up at me, looking as relaxed as I've ever seen her. I stroke a stray lock of hair out of her face, my heart beating double time.

Do I want to take her home and pound her six ways from Sunday? Abso-fucking-lutely I do. But the way she looks at me warms me from the inside out. Brielle gazes at me and her expression is… adoring. She reaches out and toys with Thorin's hair. He winks at her in his little voyeur mirror as Leo hits the brakes and throws the car in park.

Looking around, I realize we're in our driveway. How we got here, I really couldn't tell you. Leo gets out and stomps around the SUV wearing an uncharacteristic scowl. When he opens my door, I see why. Dude's hard as a hammer.

Brielle leans back, looking at him upside down. "Hello, Leo." Her voice is cheeky, but her eyes are burning.

"I just spent the last thirty minutes trying to drive while you sat back her moaning. You better get those pants up or I'm carrying you inside bare-assed."

I unclip the seatbelt and Brielle bends over in my lap to pull her pants up. Her ass grinds against my lap, and the sheer lace of her panties does absolutely nothing except make my dick leak pre-cum. I would give anything, make any promise in the world, to get inside her right now, but we wanted her in our bed.

She does something to me. To all three of us. I can't explain it, and I'm pretty sure I'd sound like an idiot if I tried.

"Goddamn," Leo groans at the sight of her, grabs a fistful of my shirtsleeve and bites his knuckle.

"Right there with ya," I mutter, trying to breathe through the ache in my balls.

Brielle turns to us with a coquettish smile. "What's the policy on teasing the doms?" She asks, her expression pure innocence.

"The policy," Leo grunts. "Is that you're welcome to try it, but it's going to get you fucked." He reaches in, hauling

Brielle over his shoulder, and heads for the front door. She grabs his ass as they disappear through the doorway.

I'd give Leo shit, but I'm no better off. I'm ninety nine percent sure these pants will be forever stretched out in the inseam.

Thorin and I follow them inside, trailing after the sound of Brielle's musical laughter. We catch up in the bedroom. The big one. We each have our own rooms, but this one has sat empty for a long-ass time. When we started on this path years ago, there was a tacit agreement that the playroom was where we brought bunnies. The rope, toys, and instruments of punishment all live there.

The bedroom just… loomed there at the back of the house. Empty. I'd gotten so used to the closed door that it just became a fixture of our lives; the physical embodiment of '*someday*'.

Thorin said the quiet part out loud first, declaring that Brielle was ours until she wanted out. And even though he caught me off guard, it only took a glance at Leo to see that he was right there with him.

I haven't been in a relationship in years. Even before the three of us teamed up, I wasn't willing to put my heart on the line for anyone. It was easy. Plenty of women wanted to try us on, but not a single one wanted to deal with the long-term logistics that make polyamory challenging. To be fair, we were never inspired to try. We were a novelty for them, and that was fine.

Until Brielle. After losing her, it hit us hard. Leo first, then Thorin. Even I caught up. It was like completing this enormous puzzle, but someone came along and yanked a single piece out of the center, carrying it away. I don't believe in luck or fate or any of that crap. But after the universe brought us back to Brielle, I'm not going to waste our chance with her. Not for anything.

So, when Leo flings the bedroom door open and tosses Bree in the center of the enormous bed, I'm right behind him.

23

LEO

Brielle peeks up at me through her lashes, and the sight of her, smack dab in the middle of the bed we've been saving, makes my heartbeat rattle my bones. I pull my tie loose, reaching back to yank my shirt off over my head. She watches with hungry eyes as Thor and Mal flank me with identical movements.

"Best. Day. Ever," Brielle says on a breathy exhale. You'd think she was a kid in a candy store the way she's eyeing us. Thor chuckles and drops his bag on the carpet. He tosses three bundles of crimson rope onto the bed, and they land right between Bree's calves. She grins down at them, a flush rising in her cheeks.

I shove my pants and boxers to the ground and climb over her, grinding my dick against her heat. She moans, lifting her hips against me. I squeeze handfuls of her ass and the curves of her hips, my mind emptying of everything but the taste of her mouth and the little moans she makes in the back of her throat.

Mallon sits on the bed. He has his arms crossed over his chest, a darkly amused smile on his face. "Are you going to have a hard time sharing, Leo?" I grin at him and roll to her other side, starting on her pearl buttons. Mal kisses her hard, swallowing ever mewl she makes. I get her top open and run my hands over her stomach.

"Fuck you're so soft," I groan, kissing Bree's belly. She lets out an adorable giggle. I give her a long, slow lick, running my tongue from her the waist of her pants up to her ribs. She shivers, moaning as she tangles a hand in my hair.

Thorin grabs the hem of Bree's pant legs, tugging them down her legs. "Give me those pretty legs, Pet." I jerk my chin at him, wordlessly asking what he's planning with the rope. "Leg ties, front cuffs."

I grin at him, an idea forming. "Well let me hold our little bunny in position for you." I lift Brielle on top of me, her thighs straddling my chest. Unhooking her bra, I toss it across the room. She takes shallow, hard breaths. I grab her ass and haul her forward. She squeaks as her knees settle on either side of my head. I bury my nose against the soaked lace of her panties, pulling the scent of her arousal into the depths of my lungs and exhaling with a groan.

"You smell so fucking good." I pull the fabric aside, watching her eyes widen and her lips part as I flick my tongue against her swollen sex. I feel Thorin adjusting the position of her legs, pointing her toes so the tops of her feet rest on my shoulders. Mallon moves behind me, pulling her hands out in front of her and working on her wrists.

Brielle's gaze darts between the three of us, but every time I thrust my tongue inside her, or suck her clit, those eyes flutter shut. I keep her distracted, driving her higher and higher while Thorin wraps and knots the crimson lengths around her thighs.

By the time he's done, I think the reality of her predicament is *just* setting in for Brielle. With her legs folded underneath her, calves and shins secured to each other, she can't lift her hips. Mal is holding her tied hands so she can't lean back or fall forward, and Thorin certainly isn't going to let her go anywhere.

She's held captive for my mouth, unable to buck or squirm. I grab fistfuls of her ass, grinding her pussy against my face and sucking her little bud between my lips. She moans, glancing over her shoulder. Thorin kneels behind her and from the way her hips jerk, I'm guessing he's got something in store for her.

24

BRIELLE

"*Oh, God-Oh, God-Oh, God-Oh, God!*" My brain isn't capable of functioning beyond that. The have me trapped, riding Leo's face and he's not messing around. His tongue, so broad and talented, laps at my pussy, thrusts inside me, and swirls around my clit.

I thought Thorin's leg ties were pretty. Pretty and pretty tame. And they might be, in any other position. But the second he took my ability to raise my hips, he turned this into an entirely different game.

Thorin watches me through those steely eyes, before lubing up his fingers. He rubs little circles around my anus, as Leo spreads my cheeks for him.

Thorin presses against the ring of muscle, slowly, patiently, but with unfailing determination. A shiver of pleasure seizes my body as he works his finger inside me. I stretch around him, but it's so intense that spots form in my vision.

"You have the sexiest ass," Thorin murmurs. "I'm going to bury my cock in it and fuck you until you can't see straight." He adds another finger, working them as deep as he can, while his other hand fists my hair, using it to pull me down harder on Leo's tongue.

Leo rumbles in appreciation, but I, unable to do anything but take all of it, shriek as the sheer ecstasy roils under my skin. "Leo — Leo please," I whisper, the tension and heat in my belly building to an almost unbearable degree.

Mal places my hands behind my head, kisses me on the forehead, and hops up, disappearing behind me. I can't tell how long he's gone, but I don't dare move my hands. When he comes back, metal glints in his hand. Thorin chuckles, and it's an ominous sound.

My clit is throbbing, my nipples aching, and I would give just about anything to come *right now*, but that doesn't seem to be the plan. Anytime I get close, Leo eases up, and every single time, I hear myself begging for release.

Thorin removes his fingers from my ass, leaving me feeling hollow. But I don't have long to wait. Something cold and smooth takes their place. It's wider, stretching me almost the point of pain, but as soon as I take a breath, he eases back, only to push a little deeper the next time.

Mal settles on the bed, a black metal chain dangling from his fingers. My core contracts when I realize what's attached to each end. He takes one of the wicked-looking nipple clamps, tugs at my nipple, and clips it on.

A swirling wave of pain and pleasure overtakes me. I'm still trying to catch my breath when Mallon fastens the second one. Leo sucks my clit, feathering his tongue against the sensitive nub as Thorin seats his toy deep in my butt. I can't move, but I struggle anyway, feeling the bite of the rope and reveling in the brutal security created by Thorin's skilled hands.

I'm so close, my body is trembling. Mallon tugs on the chain swinging between my breasts, the sensation scorching my nerves. I'm teetering on the edge of something so big that it fills me with trepidation. For a split second, I think they might actually manage to kill me with orgasms.

There's a soft click from behind me, and a split second later, the toy in my ass starts to vibrate. Mallon tugs harder on the clamps, and Leo growls against my pussy.

Every muscle in my body contracts with mind-melting exhilaration. I'm not human. I'm pure pleasure. I come and come and come. I can't stop. It comes in waves. Pulsing, throbbing, waves.

I'm vaguely aware of Leo letting up, and when the vibrations stop, strong hands lay me down on the bed. I blink up, realizing Mallon is hovering over me, his expression softer than I think I've ever seen it.

Soft fingers, so many of them, stroke my belly and breasts. They tease my thighs and caress my hips. I sigh happily as someone pets my hair, sending chills down my back.

This is an aspect of being with multiple men that I had never considered. The sexy stuff is *insane*. Brain-melting, panty-incinerating insane. But this… I've never felt so adored. I've never felt so safe or cared for. To be the center of their attention is a powerful thing.

Gentle touches feather over my nipples, not enough to really amp me back up, but certainly enough to keep warm and remind me that I haven't escaped their clutches yet. Not that I want to.

"Do you need a break, Pet?"

"God, no," I laugh. "I was promised some really specific and really filthy things." Mallon's expression changes, and I can almost see the dirty thoughts reflected in his eyes. He reaches down and unties my legs.

"You're going to need those. Come here." He leans against the headboard and pulls me on top of him, my bare back to his warm chest. Just like in the SUV, he places my hands behind his head, only this time, they're trapped. I couldn't move them if I wanted to.

Thorin hands him a bottle of lube before closing his mouth around one of the nipple clamps and running his teeth over the swollen tip. Air hisses through my teeth, making him grin up at me. Mal kisses my neck, biting and sucking at the sensitive flesh as he gently removes the plug from my ass.

"I don't vibrate," he says, humor tinting his voice as he coats his dick in lube. Thank Christ. "But I'm going to fill you up, Bree." His words roll through me, hitting at an emotional level. Not 'Bunny'. Not 'Baby'. Not 'Pet.'

"I like it when you use my name," I whisper, digging my heels into the mattress and lifting my hips. He holds my waist in a firm grip, lowering me onto him. I gasp as I feel the thick head of his cock stretching me.

"Oh, fuck," I whimper. "So big." Thorin plays with my nipples, biting and sucking, pinching and rolling. And Leo, God bless the man, stares me dead in the eye as he licks his finger, using his saliva to rub my clit.

"You can take it," Mallon whispers. "I promised to take care of you." He presses my hips back up, letting me descend a little farther. My body strains, stretching around him. "You're doing so good, Bree." His hand wraps around my throat. "That's my good girl."

My eyes roll back in my head as my butt cheeks contact his thighs. He holds my hips, and rocks up into me, thrusting gently. "So good." Mallon murmurs in my ear; a steady stream of praise interspersed with the low grunts of a man struggling to hold back.

Leo moves between my legs, leaning over Mal and me. He's so hard, the satiny skin of his dick looks stretched to its limits. His eyes are so hungry. So deep. My heart races like someone spiked it with rocket fuel, but I can't look away.

"We're going to make you feel so good," Mal whispers. "Look at his dick. If he wants you half as bad as I do, he's desperate to feel your pussy squeeze and gush all over him. We're going to make you ours, Bree."

A shiver racks my body as Leo taps the head of his cock against my pussy. He holds it in his hand, inching just the tip into my pussy with muttered profanities. "Christ, you're so tight." He shakes his head like he's unsure.

"Don't you want it?" I moan. I don't know what's taken hold of me, but I want what I was promised. I want them inside of me. I want to be so full of them that I can't breathe. One isn't enough when I want all three of them so badly.

Leo runs a hand over his face. "Baby, you can't possibly know how much." He doesn't stop this time. The thick head presses against me, and he keeps sinking. Inch by perfect inch.

I can't breathe. It's all pleasure and pressure, and when he starts to rock his hips, I feel it everywhere. Mallon groans, powering up into me from below, his hands clutching my hips like I'm his life raft.

"Thorin," I gasp. "I want you." He lets out a guttural growl, and gets to his feet, standing over me on the bed. He feeds me his cock, fisting my hair to move my mouth along his shaft.

"Fuck," Mal grits out. "Fuck, I'm not going to last. She's so fucking tight." Leo grunts in agreement, but neither of them stops. I look up at Thorin as he fucks my face. He glowers down at me, that serious expression locked in place, but the way he bites his lip and scrunches up his eyes make it pretty clear he's just trying to maintain control.

Leo and Mal move in and out of me, setting off sparks in my vision. I'm going to disintegrate or melt or come apart at the seams. It's all too much and exactly what I need. The sweat, the grunting, the hands.

"Oh, God. Oh, Bree. You're perfect… you're doing so good… fuck, you're going to make me lose it. Come for us. I want to feel you clench that tight little ass around my dick. I want you to *scream* for me."

Mal's words push me past the breaking point. It's hard and fast. Brutal and breathtakingly beautiful. The mind-numbing pleasure of it rolls over me with all the subtlety of a freight train. My body coils in on itself, imploding as Leo roars his release.

Under me, Mal groans, his grip on my hips tightening to the point of bruising as he comes. Something hot and wet splatters across my breasts, and when I can finally look up, Thorin is still standing over me, dick in hand as he leans his forearm against the wall, trying to catch his breath.

Shaking, he sinks to his knees, kissing me deeply. He rubs his cum into my skin and he makes a gravelly rumble in the back of his throat. Leo pulls back gently, helping me off of Mal.

I can barely stand my legs are trembling so badly, so he puts me back on the bed. Thorin unties my hands and pulls me against his chest. I'm sticky and sore and probably a step beyond hot mess, but I don't care.

Mal disappears for a second, reappearing with a handful of damp washcloths. Leo lays by my legs, rubbing my calves. Thorin strokes my hair. And Mallon, grumpy, gruff Mallon, takes one of those washcloths and starts at my forehead.

He cleans my face, wiping away any traces of my running mascara. He strokes my neck, cleaning the sweat from my skin. Thorin scowls when Mal cleans my chest but doesn't argue. My body floats, anchored only by their touches.

I close my eyes as Mal gets a clean towel and trails down my stomach. By the time he reaches my sex, I'm too relaxed to feel weird about it. That, and I know there's no point in arguing. Another towel works down my thighs, smoothing over the rope marks.

I should ask them to take a picture. That's my last thought before the world slips away, replaced with dreams of three big men.

I wake, expecting warm bodies, but I'm all alone in a bed that looks big enough to be two king size mattresses Frankensteined together. I sit up, groggy and sore, but still in complete bliss. Morning light filters through gauzy white curtains and I can smell coffee.

I pick up one of the dress shirts from the floor, buttoning it around me. I'm not sure who's it is, but they won't mind. As I open the bedroom door, the blissful feeling sinks. Thorin, Mal, and Leo are all out of sight, but I can hear tense whispering.

"… She'll panic. You can't just say that out loud."

"Well what else are we supposed to say? I don't think any of us can pretend…"

Pretend what? My heart sinks, my skin going icy as I creep down the hall. Their voices grow clearer, but my anxiety doesn't abate.

"So, you just want to lie?"

"It's not a lie, I just don't want her to run screaming for the hills."

Whatever it is they're talking about, I think maybe I should be included in the discussion. "It sounds like you're underestimating her again," I say, stepping out into the living area.

The three of them are huddled around a coffee table. When they see me, they all sit up straight looking guilty as hell. Three sets of eyes roam over me, but they don't speak.

I plop into a free armchair. "Don't let me keep you from your chat."

True to form, Thorin speaks first. "Mal doesn't think you can handle it."

Mallon rakes a hand through his hair. "That is *not* what I said. I just said it's…"

"Too soon," Thorin finishes for him.

"Too soon for what, exactly?" I ask leaning forward and resting my chin on my palm.

Leo stands up, pacing a couple of steps with nervous energy. "We don't want you to be with anyone else."

My heart pounds as I raise my eyebrows. "I'm not exactly in the market for another trio…"

"We want you to be ours. However that shakes out, we want you to stay. Forever, if we get our way."

Mal frowns looking down at his hands. My chest aches seeing him like that. I stand up and cross to him, curling into his lap. "If you don't feel the same way…" I meant to tell him it's okay, but the words won't come.

Because it's not. If he doesn't want me here like Thorin and Leo do, it will crush my heart into dust. Just thinking about it makes me want to cry, and I am *not* a crier.

He finally looks up, brows furrowed in alarm. "No. No, Bree. It's the opposite." His broad palm cradles the back of my head, fingers brushing my hair. "I can't let you walk out that door and wonder where you'll go. Who you'll be with. And I know that's not the deal we made. I know it's asking too much—"

I say the one thing a sub should probably *never* say to her dom. Or at least one of her doms. "Shut up, Mallon. Shut your handsome mouth right now." I can feel Leo and Thorin's eyes burning into me, and I bet I'll pay for that later, but I don't have time to be turned on thinking about it now.

"I can't imagine a world where I walk out that door and even look at another man. You're lucky I didn't sprout roots in that bed last night and flat out refuse to leave it."

A muscle ticks in his cheek as he searches my face, not quite believing me. So, I hold his face between my hands and lean in, kissing him. He kisses me back and the emotion he pours into it—into me—is breathtaking.

My heart pounds in my aching chest; my soul tugging away from it's home, trying to reach his.

When he speaks again, his voice is ragged. "I don't know if I could handle losing you."

"So, tell me to stay."

"That easy, huh?" He asks wryly.

I shrug and raise an eyebrow at him. "I'm your good girl, aren't I?"

"Mmmm… yes, you are." Mallon strokes my hair and squints at me. "But you have that bratty streak too."

I nod. "This is true. So, tell me to stay and you can spank the bratty streak out of me every Sunday."

His eyes roam my face. "Stay. Be with us. Just us. Stay and we'll spank you every Sunday before taking you to brunch."

The smile that spreads across his face mirrors the swell of emotion that expands in my chest. I grin, but bite my lip; doing my best, and failing, to keep my expression serious.

"Yes, sir."

Thank you for reading Room Thirty! If you loved Brielle and her men, check out Sugar Creek Seduction - a collection of steamy novellas. Whether you're into sexy sheriffs, grumpy lumberjacks, or kinky bosses, Sugar Creek has something for you!

Sugar Creek Seduction: Six Sinfully Steamy Novellas
Welcome to Sugar Creek, where the women are mouthy, the men are delicious, and the old biddies run their mouths at warp speed.
Easily the dirtiest small town in Maine…

One Hot Summer
When the temptation between a geology professor and his student becomes too much, they both leave town to cool off. Maybe they should have picked separate hotels…
She has him between a rock and a hard place…

Sinful Curves
Alexandra wants nothing to do with the town doctor, but a creative posting on the Curve Connections dating app might just give him the chance to prove her wrong.
He's got something under that white coat for you…

Stripped Down - Sonoma Book 1
Ever mistake a sexy contractor for a male stripper? Olive has!
Start the Donovan family saga today!

To be the first to hear about new books, sales and freebies, sign up for my newsletter here!
or visit www.maeharden.com

THE CLUB SIN SERIES

🗝 New York took your breath away, now visit Club Sin: Chicago for two more play sessions. 🗝

Fantasies are meant to come true and the men of Club Sin: Chicago will see to your every kinky desire. This June is the first play session of the year with 9 of your favorite steamy romance authors. We'll take you inside Club Sin: Chicago, a forbidden place where you'll find love and pleasure with multiple hot men in these Reverse Harem novellas. Can you handle the heat?

9 rooms, 9 fantasies…Which door will you step through?

💜 Check out the series and order your copies today! 💜

https://geni.us/ClubSinChicago1

Room Six by Ember Davis https://geni.us/NqWH
Room Eight by Penelope Wylde https://geni.us/NRxJK
Room Ten by Kameron Claire https://geni.us/01jSuw

Room Fourteen by Amanda Keen https://geni.us/M1vLkpt

Room Twenty by Jenna Thalia https://geni.us/vM8l

Room Twenty-two by Mila Crawford https://geni.us/ARXSw1

Room Twenty-four by Darcy Rose https://geni.us/bO7Bk

Room Twenty-eight by Stephanie Brother https://geni.us/qHCn

Room Thirty by Mae Harden https://geni.us/Room30

BEWITCHED BY YOU

KENNA

Crunchy rainbow-colored leaves nip at my heels as I open the back door of The Pub and step into the kitchen. The sunlight from behind me glints off the sea of spotless stainless-steel appliances and tables. Jonas looks over his shoulder at me as I unwrap my scarf. He's not much of a smiler, but one corner of his lips pulls to the side in the barest hint of one.

"Morning," he grunts, turning back to the cutting board where he's peeling a mountain of apples. Aiden nods at me from behind him, where he's mixing a batter and humming to a song playing on the ancient radio.

"Morning," I reply lightly, eyeing Jonas' back as I hang my scarf and bag on a hook in the corner. His hair needs a cut—the ash-brown curls have started to flip out from under his old ball cap, skimming the collar of his burgundy flannel shirt. I hate it when he lets it grow out because all I can think about is playing with those curls. Imagining how it would feel to run my fingers through it.

And then I picture reasons he'd be close enough to let me touch that hair…

It's distracting as hell.

I tie a clean apron around my waist, smoothing the black cotton over my jeans. "What are the specials today?" I tease, knowing damn well there are no specials. The menu for The Pub has been the same for the last decade, even before Jonas' father passed away and he took over. He'll update equipment, but the menu and the decor haven't changed one bit.

Jonas' eyes lift, meeting mine. "Oh, so you're going to be cute today?" His face is serious, guarded, but that's nothing new there, either. That's just Jonas, and even if he's giving me those stony eyes, I can hear the humor in his voice.

"I'm always cute," I retort, tilting a shoulder in his direction before grabbing pens and a notepad from the waitstaff station. Jonas makes a non-committal grunt.

Par for the course, really. Half of his communication is grunt-based, and I've been waiting tables here so long that I'm fluent in Grunt too. That one was: 'I'm not taking this conversation any further because you're my best friend's little sister and that would be inappropriate.'

I toss him a wink and head through the swinging door to the dining room, pulling chairs down and straightening the room. I cleaned it to within an inch of its life last night, and even though the tables and chairs are old, they're well maintained. Mostly. There's one that we leave intentionally wobbly for the odd tourist who insists on being seated despite our best efforts.

Locals only. That's the unwritten and creatively enforced rule that Jonas runs The Pub by. Tourists are loud, often rude, and bug the hell out of my boss. I don't care either way. I like everyone as long as they're respectful, but it's his restaurant.

I unlock the front door and straighten the sign at the hostess stand that reads 'Please Wait To Be Seated'. The locals all know to grab a seat wherever they like; this is just one more layer in Jonas' cold war on tourists.

The afternoon is quiet, and I work on autopilot, my mind wandering to the half-finished painting in my apartment. I know I need to finish it, but every time I think about it, I feel… bored. Uninspired.

I'm single and 26. I shouldn't be bored. I should be tearing it up and trying new things. Dean keeps telling me to move to New York or Chicago, or really anywhere more exciting. My move back to Sugar Creek was never supposed to be permanent, but four years later, I really can't bear to leave. I love this tiny-ass town and my adorable little cottage. And in theory, this is the ideal place for me to be creative. It's not the town's fault that I'm stuck on repeat, my life lonely and dull. I just need to *do* something.

I'm rolling silverware in the empty pub when Sutton charges through the front door. She's glowing so hard she's practically battery powered. See? I should look like that. I just have to ignore the fact that she's radiating satisfaction because she's fucking my brother six ways from Sunday.

"Kenna!" she wheedles, smiling around gritted teeth. "I need help." She bats her lashes at me like a broken doll.

"With what?" I laugh as she thumps down in a chair.

"The Wychwood Ball at the museum. I don't know how Fred handled this every year. Everything I've put together looks like a first-grade art project."

"Fred had a harem of volunteers at his disposal. I don't think he did any of the actual decorating himself."

Sutton pretends to gag. "Dear god, please don't use the v-word."

"What —?"

"My grandma is one of those volunteers."

"I don't know anyone else in the world who would call 'volunteer' the v-word."

Sutton smiles her cat-like smile. "The other word isn't a bad one. Just ask your brother."

"Gross," I say pointedly, laying out more silverware. "Fred worked his way through the bingo club, that's all I'm saying."

Sutton claps her hands over her ears. "I can't hear you! You're the creative one. Can you please just look at what we have?"

"Is this a cleverly disguised attempt to put my art degree to work?" I ask, raising my eyebrows.

Sutton holds her hands under her chin and bats her eyelashes at me. "I'll beg if I have to."

"Please don't," I laugh. "I heard you and Dean on the camping trip last month, and you were begging him plenty. It will forever be weird to hear you say, 'please'."

Sutton shrugs, not even a little ashamed of herself. I roll my eyes but we both knew I was always going to say yes.

"Of course, I'll help you."

"Oh, thank God," she breathes, getting to her feet. "Can you come by the museum after work? We'll go over everything I've done… and you can fix it."

"Sure, I'm out of here at six."

Sutton squeezes me so hard it borders on assault. "Thank you! I'll buy you dinner."

"Don't sweat it," I choke out, trying to loosen her grip on me. "Just stop strangling me with your love."

Sutton releases me, the stress gone from her face. "Never. Bonus points if you can get Jonas to let you leave early."

"I'll ask." I smile down at the silverware I'm rolling.

"Speaking of the tall, dark, and silent one... do you have a date for the ball?" She glances at him surreptitiously before raising her eyebrows at me.

"No, and I'm not entertaining this discussion right now," I hiss through gritted teeth, my smile disappearing as I glare at her.

"Pussy," she teases quietly. "You've been making eyes at him for the better part of a decade, but you're too chickenshit to say anything."

"You're one to talk," I quip back. "Took you the better part of a decade to figure shit out with my brother."

Sutton leans a hip against the table. "That was different. I wasn't pining. I was... marinating."

"That sounds dirty," I laugh.

She grins devilishly and wiggles her eyebrows at me. "Oh, it is."

"Ew! Get out of here!" I laugh, pushing her toward the door. She winks at me before calling over to Jonas at the bar.

"You're coming to the Wychwood this year, yeah? Can you keep our girl out of trouble for once?"

He lifts his chin in her direction, staying behind the bar until the door shuts behind her. Only then does he step around, joining me where I'm still rolling silverware.

"Dunno why she thinks I could keep you out of trouble," he says, voice low. His scent invades my mind and I have this insane urge to lean closer just so I can breathe him in. I don't though. My eyes wander to his hands as he grabs a fork, a spoon, and a knife, deftly rolling a paper napkin around the set. There's this quiet power in the way his fingers move. Hell, the way all of him moves.

"Could I sneak out a little early tonight?" I ask, eyes riveted on his hands. God, the things I'd let him do with those… I have a sneaking suspicion he'd be incredible in bed. I bet he's a pin-his-girl-to-the-bed-by-her-hands lover… And now that's all I can picture. His thick body rolling over mine as he holds me down, taking me hard, filling every inch—

"Anything you need, Kenna." Jonas' gruff reply cuts into my fantasy, and I shake my head, clearing it. If I told him all the things I *really* need from him, he'd fire me.

"Thank you, Jonas." I peek up at him, trying to pretend I wasn't just thinking X-rated thoughts. He doesn't need to know I'll go home and slip my fingers between my legs, wishing it was him instead.

He nods, keeping his eyes on his work. A muscle jumps in his jaw, barely visible under his short beard. He always keeps it shaved in summer, but by the time the geese fly south each fall, he's usually sporting a couple weeks' growth.

"You quit shaving already, mountain man?"

He grunts and runs a hand along his jaw, glancing down at me. "Cold out."

"That's what scarves are for," I tease.

"Don't have one," he shrugs.

"I'm not complaining." I grin up at him.

He swallows and grunts again, heading back around the bar, and I bite my lip in frustration. That's Jonas in a nutshell. If he thinks I'm even approaching flirting territory, he puts as much distance, and furniture, between us as possible.

I get it. I'm not his type. I'm too young. I'm too loud.

I'm too impulsive. *I'm Dean Carpenter's little sister.* There are probably a dozen other strikes against me that I can't even think of right now, but I know that's a big one. I'm not a viable date option, even in a town this tiny. Even though I *know* I should be used to that, it still sears through me like a hot knife.

I kissed him once, and he avoided me for three years. Does he really think I'd cross the line again and risk another exile? I don't care how many times Sutton calls me a pussy. I've learned the hard way to be grateful for the little pieces of Jonas that I get.

Sugar Creek goes hard for holidays. Our reputation for Fourth of July bonfires, over the top winter festivals, and sugar-laden Valentine's Days make Sugar Creek one of the top of the tourist destinations in Maine.

So, when I say that Halloween is a blow-out of epic proportions, I mean it. The bakery goes apple pie and pumpkin spice crazy. Store fronts are covered in cobwebs, skeletons, and massive spiders. Pumpkin arches span Main Street, and a weeklong fall festival up in the hills brings people from all over the state for apple and pear picking.

And all of it culminates in a bacchanalian costume party at the Wychwood Mansion on Halloween eve. The ball started out as polite cocktails and a silent auction, but it's come a long way in the last 20 years.

Tossing aside the puritanical values the town was founded on, the Wychwood is the one night of the year Sugar Creek citizens cut loose. Last year, the sheriff issued over 50 warnings for lewd behavior, a town record. Of course, that was before someone caught Sheriff Connor and his wife, Willow, necking in the park, their Woody and Bo Peep costumes decidedly disheveled.

I pull into the parking lot and skip up the steps of the mansion. The house was once the home of the founding family, but the historical society converted it into a town museum a couple of decades ago.

I weave through the house, looking for Sutton. I can hear her muttering somewhere.

"Marco!" I call out. There's a long pause before I hear her answering call from the back office.

"Polo!"

We call and repeat until I open a storeroom door to an explosion of black tulle and cinnamon brooms. I cough, holding my nose and crane my neck, trying to make out my friend in the disaster.

"Sutton? Are you alive in here? Or was someone experimenting with fall-themed biological weapons?"

She pops up, a witch's hat sitting on top of her red curls.

"That's a good look for you, but you're missing the wart."

"Oh, you think you're so funny," she says with a scowl.

"Play nice," I warn. "If you want me to help, you have to laugh at my jokes."

"I guess you're worth it," she sighs.

A second woman pops up from behind another box. Muriel, the museum's mouthiest volunteer and one-woman rumor mill, tosses me a stuffed cat.

"Kenna! How are you, Sugar?"

"Oh, you know, hanging in there."

"How's Jonas doing?"

I shrug and inspect the cat in my hands. "Same as always."

"So… fine as hell?" Muriel laughs, digging through another box. "The ass on that man could turn a nun's panties into a slip 'n slide."

I laugh and throw the cat back at her. She's not wrong. It just sounds so wrong to hear my grandmother's bingo buddy say things like that.

"Did you see him in that suit last week?" Muriel asks, fanning herself.

"You need to get your eyes checked," I scoff, squinting at her. "Or lay off the booze. I've known that man since I was a toddler, and Jonas Flynn has never worn a suit in his life."

"Watch your attitude, missy. The tits may have succumbed to gravity, but these peepers are still sharper than a hawk's. I know what I saw. He was scootin' out of town wearing a full-on suit. Tie and all."

"A tie?" I laugh. "I'll believe it when I see it."

We spend the evening digging through the boxes. Between the tangled string lights, mismatched vases, and odds and ends, there's enough to put together a pretty spectacular party. It's going to require a little effort and a lot of paint. It's dark by the time I cram my projects into my trunk and say goodbye to Sutton.

My car yells at me as I'm driving down Main Street. It's running on fumes and threatening to give up the ghost. I pull over at the little downtown station and fill up. An engine rumbles in the distance as the gas pump thunks off. I hop in the car just in time to see Jonas' truck pass by. My brain just about breaks when I see that he is, in fact, wearing a suit.

"The fuck…?" I whisper as I start my car. I hesitate for a heartbeat, but curiosity takes over. Instead of turning right and heading for home, I go left and follow him all the way to the edge of town.

He heads south and I trail behind him, keeping my distance until he hits the highway. Then I sneak a little closer. Too close. I'm right behind him when I catch a glimpse of his eyes in his rearview mirror.

Shit. My heart is pounding in my chest so hard I can almost hear it. Can he see me? Probably not, but I pull back, letting a couple cars get between us.

We head towards Portland. My heart rate is just leveling out when a semi-truck swerves into my lane at an on-ramp, and I have to slam on the brakes to avoid the asshole.

"Shit-shit-shit," I mutter, scanning the road for Jonas' truck, but I'm stuck behind an ancient Toyota pacing the semi for over a mile. When I finally get around them, Jonas' blue truck is nowhere to be seen. Did he speed up? Exit? Vanish into thin air? Hell, if I know.

Keep reading Bewitched by You in the Sugar Creek Seduction bundle!
Sugar Creek Seduction: Six Sinfully Steamy Novellas

STRIPPED DOWN

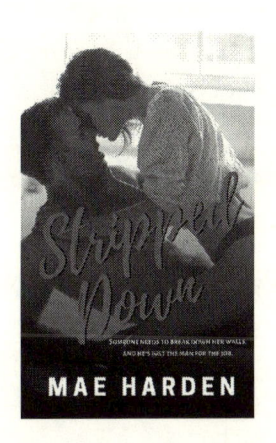

CHAPTER ONE - OLIVE

As I shepherd my friend's bridesmaids back into our hotel, I can't help but smile. This has been one of the best, most ridiculous, nights of my life. Sure, maybe sweet, innocent, virgin Chelsea should have stopped and thought about it before letting our friend (and resident wild lady) Sally plan her bachelorette activities. We've suffered no shortage of girly drinks, carousing, and penis jokes.

When we get to Chelsea's room, Sally slips into the bathroom and reappears with two bottles of champagne. I don't even know where she had those hidden. Just because she's creeping up on 65 doesn't mean Sally has settled down one bit. With her curly riot of lavender hair and a leopard print pantsuit, she led us on a bar crawl of downtown Napa. Each stop featured a different sexual cocktail along with a gift for each of us, tailor made to make Chelsea blush as hard as possible.

I met Chelsea in high school during the two torturous weeks I spent on the track team, and she's been my bestie ever since. When she asked me to be a bridesmaid, I jumped at the chance to be part of her big day. Though, I never could have predicted that a bachelorette party for someone like Chelsea would reach such epically filthy proportions.

We started with Pink Silk Panties in the hotel suite where we opened little gift bags containing pale pink thongs. The color is demure but the barely there polka dot mesh screams "Watch me strip." I'm pretty sure Chelsea's soon to be husband will pant like a dog if he catches her wearing it. Next was a round of sweet-as-shit Bend Over Shirleys and bottles of strawberry flavored lube. Chelsea blushed as pink as her drink and asked what you use flavored lube for.

Then there were the Leg Spreaders with a pair of fluffy handcuffs, the Screaming Orgasms with high-end vibrators. The Pop My Cherry shots with a full set of white bridal lingerie from Sally's boutique, complete with a little veil on the back of the white cage panties for Chelsea. The rest of us got black lingerie minus the veil. I started pumping the breaks and passing half of each drink back to the bartenders. Sugar and alcohol don't love me as much as I love them so I switch to seltzer with lime early on.

Poor Chelsea has been a flustered mess all night, Googling how to use each gift before squeaking and throwing her phone back in her purse. I've never had so much fun. Chelsea's twin cousins from Boston, Kate and Kristen, started out the night as buttoned-up as her, but with each of the dirty drinks, they loosened up a little more. The bartender at our last stop was an excellent sport, but once they started calling for more "shawts" while modeling their lingerie over their clothes I knew it was time to go. They had one too many Slippery Nipples, and it was starting to show.

It's only 12:30 when we get back to the hotel room, but the party isn't even close to over because Sally puts on some classic rock while waving her pink panties in the air. God, I hope I still party like that in my 60s. Kate is dancing on the couch but Kristen looks like she's wilting and I ask Sally if we should put her to bed.

"Don't you dare! She'll miss the entertainment!" Sally hoots over the music. Oh no. I've been friends with Sally long enough to know this can't be good.

"What entertainment?" Chelsea asks innocently.

Oh, sweet baby girl... I think to myself. "Sally, tell me you didn't." She smirks and straightens the jacket of her pantsuit.

"What kind of bachelorette party doesn't have a hunky stripper?" She looks like the cat that ate the canary.

"The nice kind," I reply. Poor Chelsea's eyes are round as saucers and she's gone pale.

"Bring in the stripper!" Kate crows from her dancing platform on the couch. Chelsea blushes so hard I'm worried she'll burn up.

Kate and Sally clink glasses and chug the remains, letting out another "Woooo!" I can't help laughing. I've never been a woo-girl but when Chelsea puts on a brave face and follows suit, pounding the last inch of her champagne I can't help but join in. It's her night.

Sally squints at the clock, "What time is it?" She asks.

"Almost 1:15."

"Damn stripper is late!" She scowls as she tries to pop another bottle of champagne, holding it between her thighs in the least ladylike display I have ever seen. There's a pounding on the door and her head whips up, lips lifting in an evil grin.

"Open up ladies! You're being too damn loud!" The voice filtering through the door is a deep baritone and one of the sexiest things I've ever heard. The festivities have gotten to me because I've never gotten so turned on by a man's voice before.

I give Sally the evil eye as I open the door. "I can't believe you ordered a strip… Oh my fucking god." The sight in front of me sends a shiver through my body.

This man is not at all what I would have expected from a stripper. I guess I was expecting a cheesy, oiled up, twenty-year-old that man-scapes and thinks he's Magic Mike incarnate. This man must be in his late 30s with a short, well-kept beard and chocolate brown hair. There's a sprinkling of silver-gray hairs at his temples. Fuck me. Why is that so hot? He's rugged and muscular in a way that makes me think he works with his hands.

His flannel has several buttons undone at the top, showing off the broad expanse of his chest, dusted with dark brown hair. My eyes drift down to his jeans, slung low on his hips and the muscular V that dips into the waistband. I know I shouldn't look, but I can't help myself because either he's stuffed a sock down his pants or that bulge promises *a lot*. I can't swallow because my tongue seems to have grown too big for my mouth.

Sexy Lumberjack leans an arm against the door frame and looks me up and down, his deep blue eyes sweeping over me, burning me. Jesus, how much did I have to drink? I'm turning to a puddle under his piercing gaze. A very wet, hot puddle. I'd love nothing more than to run my hands over his bare chest. I want it so badly my fingers are twitching, and I curl my hands into fists to stop myself.

"You ordered a stripper?" he asks. He's still wearing a steely expression, but there's a hint of a smile underneath it.

"Nuh… nah…" Holy shit, I can't talk. "You don't look like a stripper…" I start but then I throw a hand over my mouth. Was that rude? "Sorry, I didn't mean that. I mean, you look like you could strip. Obviously, you've got the body for it… I just thought strippers would have less chest hair…" Oh fuck my life. Why did I just comment on his chest hair?! I sound like a babbling idiot.

Sally saves me, calling out from somewhere behind me.

"That was me, sugar. I booked the stripper."

Sexy Lumberjack takes his eyes off me for the first time since I opened the door and smirks. "Is it just the five of you? I expected at least a dozen ladies dancing on tables from all the noise you were making."

Sally pouts. "I ordered a cop, not a cowboy. You don't even have a hat."

He chuckles, "I'm not a cowboy, I'm a contractor."

"Close enough, I guess." Sally shrugs and reaches around me, grabbing hold of a muscular arm. He lets her pull him into the room, watching me as he slides past. His body so close to mine that his bare chest rasps against the front of my dress, making my nipples pebble. It's all I can do to keep my drunk self from licking him. Drunk Me is a horny mess.

Sally jumps on the couch in her heels. "Let's see it, Mr. Contractor!" I am one hundred percent sure she will be paying damages to the hotel.

Mr. Contractor just looks at us like we're crazy. This must be his first time because he looks like he has no clue what he's doing. What the fuck is going on? I mean, I've never actually seen a stripper, male or otherwise, but aren't they supposed to come in with a boom box and props and stuff? Despite being the sexiest man I've ever laid eyes on, this guy doesn't seem prepared. Those jeans don't even look like rip-aways.

"I just came over because you're all being so loud..."

"Hurry up and strip so we can put Kristen to bed!" Kate calls out.

He cocks an eyebrow and gives us a stern look. God, that shouldn't turn me on.

GET STRIPPED DOWN NOW!

ALSO BY MAE HARDEN

Stripped Down - Sonoma Book 1

Mowed Over - Sonoma Book 2

Revved Up - Sonoma Book 3

Pent Up - Sonoma Book 4

Over Exposed - Sonoma Book 5 COMING SOON! Join my newsletter to get updates!

Sugar Pie - Sugar Creek Novella, Sweet Heart Series

Thirsty Boy - Sugar Creek Novella, Boys of Summer Series

Anyone but You - Sugar Creek Novella, Read Me Romance

Bewitched by You - Sugar Creek Novella, Halloween Steam Series

Sinful Curves - Sugar Creek Novella, Curvy Soulmates Series

Lumber Snack - Sugar Creek Novella, 12 Days of Kissmas

Sugar Creek Seduction - Six Sinfully Steamy Novellas (Sugar Creek Novella Bundle)

To Hive and to Hold - Man of the Month Club, Sycamore Mountain

Hound Dog - Love at First Bark

Room 30 - Club Sin Series, Kinky Reverse Harem

One Hot Summer - Mountain Ridge Resort, tied to Sugar Creek

COMING SOON:

Bred for Them - Sugar Creek Novella, Baby Breeders

series, MMF

Rattler & Beast - Dirty Sinners MC series, MFM

The Devil's Captive - Dark Reign Mafia series, tied to Sugar Creek

Snowed in with the Enemy - Sugar Creek Novella, Flirt Club

Wood Girl Gone Bad - Sugar Creek Novella, The Naughty List series